Cry Wolf

Aileen La Tourette

Published by VIRAGO PRESS Limited 1986
41 William IV Street, London WC2N 4DB

Copyright © Aileen La Tourette 1986

British Library Cataloguing in Publication Data

La Tourette, Aileen
   Cry wolf.
   I. Title
   823'.914 [F]   PR6062.A77/

   ISBN 0-86068-584-5
   ISBN 0-86068-589-6 Pbk

Typeset by Goodfellow & Egan at Cambridge
Printed in Great Britain by Anchor Brendon
of Tiptree, Essex

Storytelling is humane and achieves humane effects, memory, sympathy, understanding – even when the story is in part a lament for the destruction of one's fathers' home, for the loss of memory, the breakdown of sympathy, the lack of understanding.

Christa Wolf

The moment a feeling enters the body/ Is political.

Adrienne Rich

℘ Acknowledgements

Thanks to my sons Reuben and Nicholas for acting as science fiction consultants, plot advisers and invaluable listeners; to their father, my friend David Cohen, who has some, not all of those skills; to my sisters Amelie and Adele and my brothers Bill, Tim and Tom for their closeness during this period after our mother's death; to Sara Maitland who has long been both a personal and a professional influence and support; to Joan Crawford who started me off with such sound and wise guidance, still much missed; to Ruthie Petrie who introduced me to Joan, threw a memorable party and in editing *Cry Wolf* has helped me uncover my own prose style; and to Gill Saunders, difficult, inspired lover and friend.

Curie walked into the classroom. Waves of students parted to let her through, laughter and talk rolled back to offer her an aisle of silence. She walked it, then walked back again to the door, which was a simple arch. Breezes were too precious to be shut out, whatever the time of year.

Wind chimes stirred down the corridor as she pulled the curtain across the opening. The curtain was changed according to the season. This one was gold, for Autumn (One). Her favourite season. She smiled as she straightened the curtain, and felt the class relax, slightly, behind her. They were concentrating on the ritual that began the class, and on her attitude as she performed it.

Autumn was the coolest time. There was a certain tension in the air, as if invisible threads were being tightened, invisible muscles flexed. Every year Curie held her breath and prayed for reds, golds, crusty tobacco-browns. They did not come. The leaves were a pale dill-green in their spring prime, and when the thin dill liquor went back to the roots, they blanched a lustreless bone. Sometimes individual leaves bore a faint stipple of yellow.

Still there was change in the stern, sharp air, and a sense

1

of the passage of time. Memories could no more be held in check than leaves could be willed not to fall. It was planting time now, rather than harvest season. But it was what it had always been, the real beginning of the year, a time of inner planting and harvest, too, of resolution and reckoning. The old Jewish New Year and Day of Atonement had best expressed the paradox.

The growing season was speedy. Autumn (Two) incubated the first buds. Autumn (Three) fattened and teased them out into Spring (One), generally reckoned to be the vintage time of year. Buds broke, trees wore their soft dill sheen, winds hummed. Spring (Two) was mild and delectable, and Spring (Three) saw the first of the harvests.

The second followed in Summer (One). In Summer (Two) they bottled and pickled and stored the harvested vegetables and fruits. There was little enough variety, but they were unaware that there had ever been more. Except, of course, for Curie.

Summer (Three) was a season of shutdown, of aestivation. It was a period simultaneously lenten and leisurely. Sexual abstinence was observed, but work was not required, was, in fact, forbidden. Thought was almost forbidden. Torpor, mental as well as physical, was the unspoken rule. Curie had made it that way. The heat, she decreed, rendered all effort dangerous. People lounged and read themselves to sleep, woke to sip light, non-intoxicating liquids. Digestive processes slowed, along with other labours of the body.

Today they would discuss the somnolent months behind them and reflect on the busy planting season ahead, and the new harvest that would follow. Curie took a deep breath. The air had a bite to it. It seemed to her that Autumn (One) was a time of exposure, when illusions were shed from the mind like leaves. The time of exposure, of reality, was shorter now than it had ever been. A year was nine months, not twelve. There had been no winter since the thaw cracked through the ice, fifty years ago.

They would centre their reflections, as always, on the present, on Autumn (One). Each day's meditation allotted some time to past, some to future, the bulk to present. Memory and imagination were foreshortened as well as time, so that it was possible to study all three levels daily, in at least a perfunctory way. The foreshortening meant that the perfunctoriness was unnoticed. Except, of course, by Curie.

Past, present and future cannot be separated, she reminded herself. They cannot be scrutinized in isolation from one another; they do not exist in isolation from one another. But the attempt at rationalization, valid enough in itself but vapid with it, failed to convince her.

The class would lose concentration if she didn't begin soon, and it would be her fault. She was too good a teacher to allow that to happen. She turned and faced them, after a quick glance upwards at the sky, at its bluest on these first Autumn days.

'Today I wish to consider blue.' Her voice fondled the word.

'Blue *what?*' a rude voice spat back at her; but only in her mind. There were no hecklers here. They looked intently at her, cross-legged on their cushions, no one lolling in sceptical indolence. There was no scepticism here, except her own. She turned towards the curtain again to hide her face, and caught a rustle behind her. Not a hint of insurgence, she told herself. Merely a symptom of their collectively short attention span. But whether she intended to reassure herself by the mental note, or to check some dim paradoxical optimism, was unclear even to her. She swivelled to face them, closing her eyes dramatically as she spun. Her teeth clenched as she practised her nursery school teacher's tricks.

'Blue,' she stage-whispered from behind closed lids, then peeked to make sure all eyes were locked in rapt imitation. Yes. Or – wait – was there a flicker, a blue flare she just

3

caught from another peeker unlucky enough to coincide with teacher?

She pushed the impression firmly aside. There couldn't be. It was mirage, wish-fulfilment. What wouldn't she give for a spark of rebellion, for the bite of rudeness, invigorating as the new spark in the air! She bit her lip, then released it quickly. They would reflect her smallest gesture. A momentary nervous tick could become a mass deformity. She turned away to smother a grim smile. It was self-preservation, this inhibition of tiny facial contortions and muscular spasms that would once have passed almost unnoticed. To see them given back by the hundred earnest faces in front of her would drive her to distracted hysteria. She was vaguely aware that, as a result of this constant vigilance over her minutest reflexes, her body was burdened with petty tensions that would ordinarily be discharged by petty, half-conscious actions. She had to become conscious in order to abort them, and that additional self-consciousness carried the greatest tension of all.

A hundred pairs of lips, painstakingly bitten! What if she picked her nose? Or sucked her thumb? She stood stiffly, holding herself in check. She could turn them into grotesques. Any mother could turn her children into grotesques. But she, like and unlike any mother, must not. She was herself grotesque, by dint of this absurd control. But she was expected to be different. Little to choose between queen and village idiot, she mused. They have more in common with each other than with anyone else. And I am both, though neither 'village', 'queen' nor 'idiot' exist any more. But then, neither does 'mother', in its old form. And I am that, above all.

'Sky.' She turned and recited the first name in her litany. 'Remember the first sky ever seen. First blue sky. When you lay and saw it floating like a blanket.'

'Or maybe it was not the first,' she quickly contradicted herself. It was a good preaching technique. First you led

4

them up the garden path and then you did an abrupt about-face. 'Maybe the first blue is the soft, barely-blue puffball of the aureole, or the barely-blue milk, the taste of baby blue.'

She left them with that for a calculated second, then plunged in and drove them with her. Like leading horses through water, she thought, taking the reins of their plodding imaginations.

'Sea,' she said joyfully. This was still her favourite blue. There was one left, as far as she knew. One sea, out of seven. The Arctic Ocean, once more white than blue, on a spectrum from cloudy porcelain to bell-crystal. Now, without snow or concept of snow in the stolidly temperate climate that was all they knew, apart from its one steamy tropical season, the Arctic shone blue.

'Deep-blue, or green-blue,' she chanted. 'Azure or indigo. What does it speak of, what does it tell, this sea like a long letter read page after page, wave after wave, a hiss or a whisper as if invisible lips moved as the unseen stranger read, from whom does it come, the sea's long letter, and what does it say?'

She left them to ponder it. Once it had said so many things. Once it had read angrily, stormily, pages crumpled against the rocks, torn into a million fragments, broken like Moses' tablets of stone. Now it was glossy and even and calm. The small wind made a light surf, a sweet lacy foam, still, thank God, laced with salt. The sea's crackling energy was not utterly spent.

The sea's a long letter from God. That was what Curie Fairchild, Professor of Theology, wanted to say. But there was no god here. Not that kind. That way there could be no fight over whose god was *the* Holy One. That was the oldest fight, the fight behind the fights that had first banked the snow and turned the waves into crystalline combs, frozen upright in the iced-over seabed in the attitudes in which the wind had caught them.

'Blue,' she pronounced sternly, to shepherd her own

5

stray thoughts and any other wanderers'. She turned again to the curtain, to make sure that no agitation betrayed her. Not that they could guess the cause. The world as morgue was not an image they could comprehend.

'The sea. A long letter. A love letter,' she said softly, thinking of the morgue-world all the while, with its sheets of dry-ice smoke rising from the naked blue forms. There were no clothes to spare for the dead. 'The sky, the sea's mirror – or is it the other way round? Who can say? Or is the sea the sky's own unsigned letter?'

She waited again. Let them contemplate that. Once the sky traced shapes and scenes, she could have added, it was a stage, a seat of drama and farce, a gallery hung with pictures from every school. But such fanciful notions would have no meaning for them. There were clouds, still, rainclouds which gathered regularly, almost dutifully, in sullen unsuggestive blobs. They poured down the ration of water necessary to grow the few kinds of foodstuffs and trees left, and then dissolved. The trees and vines and shrubs grew readily enough. There was simply a meanness in the lack of variety she could no more explain to these children of want than she could tell them the source of their world's limitations.

> Allow not nature more than nature needs,
> Man's life is cheap as beast's –

But they didn't notice the limitations. Nature's blunted and abbreviated needs were all they knew; and their own.

'Rain, with its blue shine,' she instructed them. 'Rain, with its blue tune,' she dared. Would such a metaphor mean anything to them? She sensed their puzzlement, but decided to go on.

'Sadness,' she said gently. 'A blue feeling.' She had allowed them to know sadness. How else could she live among them? But not too much, for the same reason.

'A blue feeling. Before night, before morning. In between. Lost, a little. Left out in the rain, even in the sun. Left out. Blue.'

6

She hummed a tune. 'Blue tune like the rain,' she hummed again, let her voice swell, become a wail. Once the earth turned blue. The planet could not draw breath. There was only dry ice, smoke, and thirst. But there was no water, only ice to suck, tiny shards of it, burning the tongue. The only way to survive was to suck it all the time, to live with your blackened mouth on fire while the rest of you slept, limbs tucked foetally, piled like kindling for a sacrifice. You were the sacrifice, and the fire. Then the thaw came, and with it pins and needles as though an angry god stabbed voodoo dolls in the heavens, enraged by the futile, profane mockery of such burnt offerings. Many could not endure the pain of fiery, ice-sucking half-sleep, let alone the pain of waking.

She sang on, wordlessly. It was her one real release. She could give them music and divulge nothing. All her secrets were in the blues line she wailed at them without giving anything away. Something else that had survived: the blues.

But she had to stop, before the words forced her lips. She stopped abruptly, another good tactic, and went on to the eroticism of blue.

'Blue lines the pockets of the body, where the treasures are,' she prattled. 'The little pebble of the clitoris to suck, the nib of the penis to fill.'

Their attention came easily now. The difficult part was over.

'The armpits and inner thighs, the earlobes, in between fingers and toes,' she chanted. 'Behind knees, between buttocks, elbow-bends, lips, the dusk of the circles beneath the eyes,' she crooned, putting her voice and her mind on a sort of automatic pilot. She could itemize blue features like this in her sleep. Or green, or red, or any other colour. Sleep was the next blue subject, she reminded herself. Blue slumber and dreams. Their dreams were less aggressive than puppies', not that there were puppies now. Blue skies and

7

fields of daisies. Well, if you had to have only one kind of flower left, let it be one with a diversity of types to fit all your sermons, or lessons, or whatever. They treasured their daisies, she had to admit. They would never dream of pulling off petals.

Lazy Susans, gold and brown, yellow daisies, pinks, whites, reds. A humble thing that had remained. Sometimes she cursed them for being the only kind. Fatuous silly grinning daisies. Unscented. Just as she hated herself for being the only one left of her kind, just as she cursed her own fatuous life.

'Blue nights,' she sighed. 'Blue fire. Blue desire. Part of the sadness of blue is desire, that is filled and always revives and revives and so is never filled – or does not revive, and so dies.' Death was next on the list.

'It's too bad you have such a way with words,' said a voice from the deep, far past, and a faraway child-Curie frowned as if in surprised incomprehension, though she knew very well what was meant.

'It stops you learning anything,' the voice said with amused regret. 'You get caught up in your own circus act with words, and you never get down to it. And you take everyone else along with you,' the voice concluded, with an audible smile.

Miss Kirkwood, a teacher, far along. Kirkwood far along, that is, not Fairchild; far along in time and truth, while Fairchild her student (the 'fair' in Fairchild was a reference to beauty and not to justice, and had remained so) was nowhere, then and now, polishing and perfecting the rhetorical skills and tricks her long-ago teacher had so tolerantly deplored.

Where would I be now without them, she asked the long-dead Kirkwood, in her head. Eh?

In the stalwart silence, she regarded her class. Some of them would see, or claim to have seen, a blue aura or haze or nimbus around her. Some would see her very skin glow

8

blue. Oh, irony! Another voice from the past said: 'I've had enough bloody irony to last me forever.' But it never stopped.

They were eminently suggestible. She had floated and flown in the classroom before, or so it was said. Once, she glinted darkly, she'd have been burnt as a witch. Tonight she would be said to have metamorphosed into a cloud, into the essence of blueness, like the tigers running round the tree into butter – or was it pancakes and butter, and anyway, what a racist historical memory! She shook herself. She was Curie, Professor of the Sem of the Gods of the Body. Their cult. Her cult. *The* cult. She glanced at her watch; she still had death to do, before they wrote their own ideas.

She sniffed at the thought, then began. 'Shadows,' she purred. 'All blue. Shadows accompany light. No light without,' she reiterated emphatically, and then suddenly, her will crumbled. Her own fraudulence overwhelmed her. How could she prate of light and shadow to these innocent monsters, how could she? 'Endings,' she managed. 'Blue nebulous spaces. Possibilities, ghost-shapes, back to the beginning.' She turned her back decisively to indicate that her performance was over. It was now up to them to do their best with *blue* in their pictographic writing, in their childish notebooks, more like scrapbooks.

Once she would have been refreshed by her own tricks. Now she felt as stale as though she, not them, had been propped in front of a TV screen, watching a rerun. She had bored herself – blue.

But they knew nothing of boredom, or TV. They bent over their babybooks writing babyishly. They were so clumsy, so easily dazzled. They made her want to weep, and she must not.

They bowed before they began, acknowledging her magic. She bowed back with an irony totally lost on them, and they bent in concentration. That's the point of all education, she told herself weakly; like prayer. To bring about a state of

9

profound concentration. All learning is learning to pay attention.

She was as self-sceptical as she had been over her earlier rationalization concerning the trite, tripartite way she conceptualized time for them. Pap, she gave them pap, chewed and mulched and gummed till it was thin and tasteless. And they didn't know the difference; they had never tasted anything else.

One face lifted as if to contradict her. Not 'as if'; one face lifted to contradict her. One pair of eyes was raised up from the childish, old-fashioned notebook (old-fashioned to her eyes, but not to theirs, that knew nothing of fashions more than fifty years old) to stare at her, and not in awe or gratitude either, for the revelation they had just received at her behest; no. In criticism. Almost, Curie felt, in condemnation.

We are not children, the (blue) eyes said. But these are children's games, children's tricks. *We* know nothing else. But you do. You do. You do. The eyes burned their maddening insistence at her, insisting like a child, by repetition. That was how she knew the blue look was not a figment of her own guilty imagination.

'Sophia.'

She must speak. The look was a challenge. Sophia could know nothing of challenges, or of condemnation, yet they were there in her eyes, and could not be ignored without risk. She could certainly know nothing of guilt, and yet the sense of what her eyes gave out fostered Curie's guilt as if she knew it was there to be fostered. Where had she learned the old instant nightmare of eyes and guilt?

Wherever, however, the gauntlet of that blue gaze had been flung into the air. Curie must answer the challenge, though she alone, she knew, had registered it. If only she might believe she was exaggerating the significance of that stare. If only she could imagine that she had imagined it, out of fear and concomitant hope. The fear was justified, the hope was not.

10

The blue eyes flashed again. Curie almost smiled. It was just Sophia's luck to have eyes colour co-ordinated to this day of her rebellion. She had style, and spirit. Perhaps they were the same.

Stop fiddling with rubbish theology, she scolded herself, instead of looking a political reality in the eye. Her ancient fault, older than the world she shared with these intent children bent double over their paper. Their spines were more supple, or less vertical, at any rate.

Jellyfish, she derided them and instantly knew two painful blades. The old blade of guilt, probably rusty by now from immersion in her own blood, and as if an antidote, another sword-flash of blue from Sophia, cutting across her instantaneous remorse as though she had heard what preceded it.

Jellyfish! The look said. And, pray, what might that be – and pray, who made us what we are, and why? How dare you insult your own offspring, might as well say your own invention!

She walked towards Sophia, deliberately slowly. She must still this treacherous hope that was the most dangerous emotion she could know. It came from the loneliness, the lonelinesses big and small, the loneliness overall. No one else had ever heard of jellyfish, or knew that her own backbone was deformed, or devolved, if you wished to be polite about it. They didn't even know what those words meant. Ignorance feeds on itself like knowledge, she'd discovered. If you keep people in ignorance they will grow in ignorance, they will cultivate a giant ignorance of their own, beyond your wildest dreams. And beyond that shrinking horror at the spectacle of so much ignorance, there was the spectre of her loneliness, the loneliness of all her unshared knowledge and experience; was there a difference? And the vain, stupid hope that someone might know.

'M-other,' Sophia intoned the traditional salutation at

her approach, with just the merest trace of irony in her tone.

'M-other,' Curie gave back firmly.

They were all M-others, three syllables in one breath, male and female, young and old. They were born maternally responsible for themselves and their planet. It was the only title that existed in the Gods of the Body, the only form of address they knew. It covered everything. Infantile need and the yearning that survived infancy and lasted to the grave were expressed in that first fundamental consonant. Then the hesitation, a little bridge between the two most difficult realities. The space, the hesitation, between self and other, the pause to acknowledge and experience a separation, a separateness, and then the longer part of the address, the vast, definitive 'other'. It was ingenious, except of course that it had never been explained. The explanation was impossible, given the sea of ignorance, and the lack of backbone of these jellyfish-creatures.

'M-other,' Curie repeated, and inclined her head in the direction of the arched doorway with its pulled-back curtain.

Sophia rose in one graceful movement, ironic even in obedience, and led rather than followed Curie out of the classroom.

Curie's thoughts were a turmoil she fought to keep from registering on her face. Let Sophia experience only a conflict that began and ended with herself.

I am thinking in decrees now. Curie swallowed. I resent walking behind her. What madness, what megalomania afflicts me, and have I remained unaware of it only for the blindest of reasons, because I have always been met with unquestioning obedience, before?

The thoughts she was attempting to suppress swarmed and diffused her self-accusation. As if, she mused, adding to the confusion with yet another layer of thought, I think ever more densely as their thoughts fan out and thin. She added to the array of her own mental images the spread of a hinged fan, painted with pretty water-coloured pictures, like the images she had delivered to them that very morning. And behind all these spinning thoughts and images, she had the dolorous notion that had begun the process of repression and masking: that the skip or space in their title, M-other, was precisely the space of a strangled sob, a catch in the throat.

There was self-disgust for the sentiment written on her face when Sophia turned around in the softly aerated corridor. The other students had not even marked their exit from the classroom, let alone begun to notice Curie's agitation, let alone begun to scan her thoughts as her absurd fear and far more absurd hope had led her to believe Sophia might scan them.

'You are tired, M-other,' Sophia said now, with real concern. All inquisition was gone from her face. There was only love left.

Curie felt breathless. How could her student change so fast, undermining the masks and the necessary, the essential repressions? She clutched at the reprieve of illness and nodded weakly, fluttering her eyelashes.

'I shall walk you home, M-other,' Sophia said decisively, in response to the weakness, or the eyelashes, or both, and turned on her heel.

Curie felt distinctly dizzy. To try to counteract her dizziness, she somersaulted herself from the nearest window instead of following Sophia in orderly procession down the hall. She would not be marched by this blue-eyed warden from her own seminary.

'Very impressive, M-other,' Sophia said drily. 'If you like that sort of thing.'

Curie jumped, more breathless still. How had Sophia got there so fast, under the window? She moved like a cat. Not that she knew what a cat was. Curie hugged her lonely secret knowledge to herself, gloating like a miser over the hoard in her mind that made her so invincibly superior.

13

'Curie!' The young voice rang out sternly. 'Lean on me, for the sake of your body's gods.'

It was an inescapable command, one that could be read on two levels. As a medical order, it meant that whatever it prescribed was to be followed to the letter, lest the prescribee risk injury, in their cult tantamount to blasphemy, when it was courted and culpable. As a spiritual injunction it meant the physician doing the prescribing had noted a potential blasphemy against a spirit that inhabited that body along with its gods, in this case against the spirit of humility. But how could Sophia have detected Curie's arrogance, without reading her thoughts?

She leaned obediently and let Sophia pull her towards her own compound. She wanted home like a sick child, as if her somersault had full-circled her from her alternately sad and contemptuous castigation of her class's childishness to a sudden sharp experience of her own. Such self-administered lessons often occurred, she had noticed before. She almost felt better, identifying one now.

'You feel more in control and therefore better,' Sophia said shrewdly. She used no title, which underlined the fact that she had just called Curie by her name. It was not exactly a liberty, not exactly a familiarity, but something both less and more, in their scheme of things.

Given who I am, it virtually amounts to a proposition, Curie acknowledged. The last thing she needed now was the sort of sexual whiff from Sophia, or from herself towards Sophia that she had so severely pinched off in the past.

Sophia smiled. Her grip loosened and lengthened.

Curie walked steadily on. She would cultivate ignorance. That was the safest response to this nonsense. She had no notion what Sophia was up to. Probably mere puerile mischief, a childish crush on teacher. The rest was her own fantasy, and she must quash it.

In her fantasy, Sophia was born with a sense of the three missing months and the other truncations they symbolized

14

and presided over by their very absence. Curie alone, of them all, had a keen sense of loss, like the mirage impression of an amputated limb. The others were amputated, but without sense, permanently anaesthetized. Most dangerously and strikingly of all, it was as if Sophia shared that aching, amputated sense of imagination and memory, the two most stunted faculties.

It was impossible. It was a mirage in the desert of loneliness. It was lust. It was dirty-old-womanhood, which could strike even a withered theology professor. Sophia was her best student, after all, her prodigy.

It is time to retire, Curie told herself emphatically, as they tramped the fields between the Sem and her bungalow. The fields were stripped, ready for planting. Memory invades and escapes now, amidst all this emptiness, in phrases and images I almost allow to escape me in turn. That must not happen. I must go and live among the mystics, as I have longed to do for so long; for the whole of my unnaturally long life. Or for all my long, unnatural lives. There have been many. Let there be one more, shorter than all the rest, and simple, at last. That is what I mean by natural. What else? If simplicity does not belong to human life, then I shall lead another sort. Perhaps that is what the mystics do.

Let me go now, in Autumn (One), while the fields are bare and I can see. 'Pack up my little gods and go' – where does that come from? Another life. Make reality mine before it eludes me again. This I can recognize, and must claim.

She longed for sleep, and beyond sleep, for death. Maybe it was winter in the grave, she conjectured. Or in the other world; Dante's inner circle of hell was ice. But surely there would be no room left in that inn for a petty sinner like herself. Not when the indifferent whom Dante consigned there, the button-pushers, had been so many and so deadly. Dante! What made her mind wander so? Exhaustion, no

15

doubt. Such a tour-de-force as she had mounted this morning, capped by her foolish somersault over the windowsill, were expensive at her age. It was no joke, preaching to the converted. The boredom of it could be terminal.

'Come, M-other, to bed,' there was no lasciviousness in Sophia's voice, only concern and concerned anger. 'You should not waste so much energy in showing off,' she scolded, helping Curie off with her sandals.

'Now you look here,' Curie began indignantly.

'Lie down.' Sophia pushed her down, none too gently. 'You can scold me when you've caught your breath.'

Again the title, the traditional 'M-other', was conspicuous by its absence. Sophia had broken from the ranks and mounted somewhere else, somewhere meant to be inaccessible to all but Curie. Paradoxically, this gave Curie a whole new perplexity to deal with in the matter of her succession.

The succession, Curie corrected herself. It is not mine. I even talk to myself in decrees, she sighed. And will no doubt go on doing so in retirement. But that's all right. I can tell myself to go to hell, to the innermost circle, to winter. They can't even swear.

She had neglected to teach them. She thought too much and said too little. She had no choice. She could no more stop thinking than she could voice her thoughts. But the pressure of all those unspoken thoughts created tension, like the tension of her unfinished gestures, her inhibited tics. One day the tension would explode and destroy the carefully re-created world. And then what?

No, no, she must retire. But how could she retire without an heir? Sophia was to have been her heir. And now Sophia was breaking rank and discipline, was belittling and blaspheming, was, above all, refusing to behave with the exaggerated, conspiratorial courtesy of an heir apparent.

'I don't know how you can live here,' Sophia hectored as she pressed a cold compress onto her forehead. 'With no canopy.'

16

A canopy was a ceiling of fern trees. There were five varieties of tree left, all tropical or semi-tropical. The shrunken woodland was less a mock-forest than a mock-rain forest; infinitely more mocking, with a mere five inhabitants where once there had been an infinity. There was the tough, resilient palm, the ancient carob, whose weights they used, and enjoyed in the using, like children playing a game; the coconut, the fig, and the fern, grown into a tree, now, that topped the others and wove a fishing net for the stars. There were far fewer of them, too.

'I like the Wasteland,' she said, smiling feebly. All her private jokes were so entirely private. Then she sat upright and looked out of her open window, curtainless like the classroom window at the Sem.

Even in her mortified state, ashamed to show weakness and especially to show it to this half-enemy, half-seductress, she relaxed against the pillows Sophia had propped. Her back hurt. But she must have a look out over the barren stretch of land she allowed herself a real attachment to. An acknowledged attachment, was more accurate. Who could say how many unacknowledged but all-too-real attachments remained to her?

'You like it, don't you,' Sophia said with affectionate disbelief, casually sinking down beside her.

Too casually. Curie pulled herself up again, at the price of another bolt of agony, and spoke more stiffly.

'Yes.' She pronounced it with dignity. As if she had to justify her preferences to this snippet, this changeling, who even in her mysterious hunt, chasing something she either sensed in Curie or missed in herself, or both, was infinitely less prescient and alert than the daughters of the before-time, or Curie herself.

'There you go again,' she sat up in turn, jolting Curie. 'You always have to defend yourself against me with that pride, that irascible superiority, don't you?'

17

Where did she get such language? The vocabulary taught, or, literally, dictated by the Gods of the Body was limited and simple. 'Irascible' was simply not included.

'Why do you waste so much time?' Sophia went on. 'Never mind the wasteland, you can love that if you must – what of the waste time? How can you choose, and waste, that?'

'What do you mean, Sophia?' Curie's old professionalism came to her aid. Her voice was silky. She was dealing with a personnel problem, not a personal problem. 'Why do you call it waste? What do you not do that you wish to do?'

'To do, to think, to be,' Sophia was breathless, now, with rage. 'You know I do not know what it is. I only know that it is, and that you know. You know.'

The two women stared at each other. Curie was dumbfounded. She was staring at an equal. Such a stare as that would exist only in photographs; but there were no photographs, thank God. God?

'We make wind chimes, we draw, we write,' Sophia went on passionately. 'All things that children can do, and yet we are not children. *We are not children*,' she repeated in a low, intense growl, then as if she felt all efforts of mere voice projection were of no avail, she sprang up and stood over Curie, on the bed.

'I am not a child,' she said in a low, loaded voice. 'I am not.'

'Why not go on and stamp on me, destroy me, to prove it, Sophia,' Curie answered. There was murder in those blue eyes now. It was a long time since she'd looked at murder. She had dared to hope her own death would look down, or out, from different eyes.

'No,' Sophia hunched on all fours over her body. 'Because it would die with you. That which you know would die with you, and be lost to us.'

It will die with me anyway. It is lost to you now. Curie kept herself from speaking aloud what would have been the

18

admission that Sophia was working for, goading her to-wards. Right now Sophia had to be pushed off, away. She, Curie, required space and silence. That was all. She did not even rebuke herself for thinking in decrees.

'I am unwell,' she said into the steely blue eyes so close to her own. It was a sexual and spiritual excuse. 'I am unwell and I am going to Potter's Field to walk and rest and bathe. You may tell the others, and I shall see them there for Eventongue.'

Sophia pulled herself away with a defeated jerk. She knew she had overplayed her hand. She was also embarrassed by something that could have been her own tremor of desire.

'M-other,' she said, and darted out of the door.

The pause in the word was a tear-space that time, for sure, Curie acknowledged with a pained smile. Sophia had left as if she never expected to meet Curie again. But that was ludicrous. She was simply an over-dramatic young thing, that was all. Murder and mayhem indeed, and in deed, not, but only because 'It would die with you'.

Her smile froze. Indeed. She remembered those eyes, that turned from slate to steel to velvet, petal-velvet, by an exercise of skill or guile that far outmanoeuvred her tricks of the morning, or so she felt, at least in the effectiveness of their blue changes on her.

Am I merely jealous, then, because she can change the colour of her eyes as they say I can change the colour of my aura, which I know is rubbish. Would it be green, now?

She considered. Sophia crouched above her, breathing hard. Was it passion, would the wretched aura be red?

'Oh, bother auras, or aurae!' She stuttered to the scrub-land. Her eyes warmed at the sight of it, not for the late sun that splotched and showed its myriad mounds and wrinkles. Trees and daisies held little charm any more, she reflected. They were for people without memories, without imagin-ation. She needed only to quiet and contain her own. The scrub was their kennel.

19

A laugh broke from her as she plopped back down on the bed, and she stopped the hand that was about to stifle it. Why? I'm tired. Let me laugh. Dimple like a girl, climb down another rung of the grotesque towards – what? Who cared? Sophia couldn't see. No one could see.

Sophia had the same austerity as the scrubland. Too bad Curie hadn't thought to mention it when she was challenged for preferring the bleak plot she inhabited to the canopies elsewhere.

'The better to see you in, my dear,' she should have said, 'And besides, such dryness, such rocky, relentless land-scapes, resemble you, like a reflection of your soul.' She might have got herself throttled after all, and solved all problems, present and to come.

The principal of the Sem ruled the world. What was left of it, of course, but that wouldn't bother Sophia, because she couldn't compare. She had no basis, and anyway, *anyway*, comparison was unknown, untaught at the Sem. Comparison, the Founding Mothers had decided, was the root of all evil, or one of them. They were always finding new ones, and which one was the taproot became impossible to say.

But she compares herself with me, I know she does. Curie padded to the sink in the corner of the room that always made her feel as though she lived in a hotel, and splashed her face with water.

'Blue,' she said caustically to her reflection in the mirror. It was a shadowy reflection, cast on glass with black cloth behind it. The five Founding Mothers of GOB were un-certain about mirrors.

But it was the shadows in her mind that concerned her. This was no ordinary day! No wonder Sophia had bade her rest, like a child preparing for a rare late night. Tonight was the late night of the year, the fertility festival. The major festival, the planting-time fittingly celebrated with the reverend members of GOB firmly planted inside each other, in the style and manner of their inspired choosing.

And she had forgotten it! Had Sophia perhaps noticed, after all? She'd have scolded or taunted or attacked me with it, Curie reassured herself. Taken over immediately on grounds of mental instability. And she'd have been right.

But I don't want her to take over, on any grounds. She sank down on the bed. Sophia would think, along with the rest, that the morning's virtuoso performance had been an unofficial opening of the festival. Her sanity was safe, by reputation at least.

The babies were planted now, and born at the end of Spring (Three). Six months' gestation instead of nine. Two months to feed them up before they, too, fell into an obedient daze during the heat.

Obedience. How could she continue to command it? On the other hand, they need never know about her memory lapse. They would assume that her 'blue' performance anticipated the festival in some way they could not quite fathom but would accept with their usual blind faith. They would wait for her to explain, and if she did not explain, they would accept that, too. They would never guess. Even Sophia had not guessed.

She could not repress a pleased smile. Then it congealed on her face. Sophia had guessed something far more important. Sophia had winkled into her fossilized brain sufficiently to detect her arrogance, her base pride, the pride she was demonstrating to herself right now, instead of abasing herself before –

Before whom? What god or gods? The former was dead, and she had, herself, invented the latter. Not single-handedly, it was true, but she could not bear to think of her dead companions, much less to worship them. That degree of concentration, of attention to what was so very gone, would destroy her.

But she stood and stared out the window, remembering

21

how they had stooped to the dirt, rubbed it to mud with water, baked it in the sun to build their world. They had only earth and water and sun. 'Only natural ingredients', they'd joked. It seemed incredible now, that they'd joked. But it had been necessary, then as now.

It was like a little Spanish settlement, adobe at least, if lacking the wrought iron. One more thing to miss. Abruptly, she reached up and pulled the liturgical gold curtain to. Why encourage such thoughts, such maudlin reminiscences and transparent regrets? Better to lie back on the bed, and prepare to make a decent showing at the festival. She watched the crosshatch shadow of the curtain on the wall. No more tic tac toe in the world either. That, too, was made of competition and aggression, in its petty, puny way. Better not to allow such things even in such miniature forms. 'Because thou hast been faithful in small things, thou wilt be faithful in large –'

'Who said that,' she sat up to ask, accusingly, as if she expected an answer from the scrubland, or beyond.

None came. The light wind blew, the curtain barely shook. She shrugged down again. There had been so many writings and writers, prophecies and prophets. Now there were none.

'And a good thing, too,' said Davy's unmistakeable voice, conversationally. She could be conversational about her atheism, because it was hers. Until it wasn't, anymore.

Oh, Davy, where are you now, Curie sighed, burrowing into her bed; but this time there was no looking round for the source of the voice. She knew it came only from herself. She had learned that you didn't lose the dead, from your own constellation of love. But their light changed. It became a pulse, a flicker, like the twinkling of stars that came from long ago, and for the same reason; because the past was its source, because what you saw was what had been. But it was nonetheless real as you saw it, as everyone knew when they stared at the stars, and felt time itself shiver and dance.

22

'Dance' reminded her of the festival, which reminded her of Sophia which, she realized on the edge of sleep, brought her back full-circle to the strong pulsebeats from the past that meant Davy, who distinctly resembled Sophia. Or vice versa, depending on how you looked at it.

Curie woke as if from a dream. But there had been no dream, none that she remembered. She dressed for the evening, trembling at the thought that she might have worn her ordinary clothing, confusing the calendar, throwing off the year. Destroying the order. Then she remembered the afternoon's ordeal with Sophia, and her trembling made her sit down again.

Where had Sophia learned such things, such words? She had spoken and acted with an abandoned hatred Curie had never seen, not in this world, not in this incarnation, and she, Curie, had responded to it and spoken to it as if in the old, in the language of the old. What did Sophia know of murder when there was no such thing here?

Sophia never used that word, Curie reminded herself. Nor did I. All I said was 'destroy'. But she understood, she countered herself, she refused the destruction because knowledge would die with me if she agreed to it. She understood murder, whether or not she knew the word. Murder has entered the Body.

What was the antidote? Murder Sophia. A demon whisper suggested it, but she brushed it away. It was no more serious than a fly. What was serious was this sense of climbing through sand while she watched her feet touch down on plain tiles, this feeling that she lived a dream while she knew she woke and walked in wakefulness. How could she tell, with certainty, that she had not dreamt the encounter with Sophia on her bed? Dreamt it out of hatred or out of love, what did it matter? It was maddening not to know. She must step down from her position of authority before she became mad, that was certain. But whom would she appoint in her place?

I must disappear and take my secrets with me. She completed her preparations. The old, scorched face, so different from the other faces. So much more like the faces she would encounter now, in the Field, the graveyard. Despite her burdens, she looked forward to her walk. There would be time to spend alone in the Field, before the others came.

Maybe that was the cause of the hunched backs of the long-ago old. Maybe they hunched and strained under the weight of accumulated thought and secret sorrow, secret in their case simply because it was impossible, ever, to share, and they knew it. 'A sorrow shared is a sorrow halved' – but there was no sharing of sorrow, or even of joy. Perhaps either, unhalved, could crab a walk, hunch a back.

With that bleak hypothesis for company, she walked towards the Field in the late afternoon light. Her favourite light. Sophia had accused her of keeping secrets unhatched like eggs denied movement and life. They would die with her, her chicks. They would never emerge from her shell, her unspeakable secrets.

The Potter's Field was a beautiful place. She had wanted that, as though to make restitution to the unburied millions or to the un-named Companions who had helped her design it and lay there themselves, un-named. Where there were names there must be histories to accompany them, and the Founding Mothers had decreed that there would be no history. They had agreed, they had decreed. It

25

was only now that she alone was left to carry out their unanimous decrees, that there was guilt in the miserly hoarding of history. They had thought to extinguish guilt.

They called it Potter's Field not so much as a desolate joke as a piece of logical conclusion, a place of logical conclusion. What better name for a resting place in a cluster of dwellings made entirely of sun-baked clay? What better acknowledgement that they were all just sun and water and mud, that they were poverty-stricken beyond reckoning, and equal, at last, in their poverty?

They had arranged the way of death for the Gods of the Body first, before they theorized or analyzed or thought out anything else. It hadn't occurred to them, by then, that making death their first priority was morbid. It simply was their central reality. Once upon a time it had been hidden and obscured, almost denied. That had done no good, had led to other denials. Let it remain real, let it be seen. Let everyone in on the secret from the moment they were born.

It was another feature of the body they worshipped. It was that body's destiny. As such it must be respected. One must shake hands with it, more than once, before it came for the final embrace. One must have at least a nodding acquaintance with it.

How strange they would have found us, at one time, Curie thought as she entered the green vine-gates of the Field. They'd say we fetishize it. Perhaps we do, perhaps that is the only way to comprehend it.

Perhaps there is no way to comprehend it. They had tried to avoid mystery, in the end, to explicate and tame in an effort to overload the machinery of fear with the facts that, they thought, would jam it. Maybe they were naive after all their vast experience.

She stooped to examine a small plot, and smiled. There was a little altar on it, a very primitive one, that reminded her of the roadside shrines of long ago. This one was a Heart altar, bearing a heart sculpted of mud, of course, and painted red and blue. Blood and transcendence. Blood and blood, she corrected herself; blood comes in red and blue. The flowers were red, too, and little. A child's grave, from the looks of it.

There was no need here for anyone to inquire of a child, 'What will you be when you grow up?' They were all the same. Everyone was a religious, a paramedic, a parent. There were no other choices. Everyone tilled and harvested, everyone baked bricks and built buildings, everyone did everything.

Besides, there was no growing up for many children. There were so many sudden, unexplained deaths that such a question would have been considered the worst of cruelties. They lived in the present, Curie reminded herself, with a glance at the recent past and the near future, because that was itself more than they were certain of.

She felt better about her qualms of the morning. How else could time be taught to them, when their expectations of it were so humble, when each child born in GOB spent a little time each day, from the age of three, planning and planting what would be her grave?

To live close to the earth was to live close to death. Once only select groups of monks had known that, or at least lived it. Monks with skulls on their tables, she remembered, considered lunatics. They had lived better than most, probably, within their lights.

A better question for the M-others was, 'What will you be when you go down?' They would appreciate the double entendre. 'Going down' was a slang phrase for sex in GOB, culled from whatever linguistic memory, from some remnant of American slang, she supposed. Immediately it flashed upon her that Sophia's grasp of more than the concept of murder might come from a similar anomaly. They had planned a civilization without history. If that couldn't be called a civilization, so much the better! The name had meant nothing in the past, let them live without

27

it. They had plotted a society without history, then. But perhaps some memories, like some words, like some ideas, were carried in the body itself, the body whose word was law.

'What will you be when you go down?' She'd rather think about that. 'Pregnant'! That would do for après-sex and après-death as well. Pregnant with dreams that stirred and kicked; for all acts of love engendered those. And then with earthworms. Maybe she should introduce the joke.

Her time for introducing words or jokes was over, she reminded herself. GOB would be spared that particular one. For years she had woken from sleep with a thrill of energy, because a dream had inspired her with another invention. When you started from scratch, there were so many things to invent. Words, jokes, expressions, even stories that could be carried word-of-mouth. The range of tales was limited by the understanding of the listeners. But she skilfully scooped out the centre of fairy tales and folk legends, and gave them the soft, sweet surround.

At twelve the grave was confirmed, its place made permanent, its design celebrated. At sixteen there was a last chance to alter it, for those who lived to be sixteen. Some of the gardens were elaborate and some were crude. Most were crudely realistic shrines with moulded clay hearts or brains or limbs to honour the individual cults that made up GOB. Curie shuddered. The effect of the dark emblems was eerie. The Field was like an archaic battlefield strewn with vestigial relics of the dead.

But green pressed close to the little representations and often obscured them, as did flowers. It was disconcerting not to be able to distinguish the graves of the living from those of the dead. There were no names, that was another feature of the Field. No names for anyone, no individual histories. Theirs was a tribal consciousness. The single individual form of self-expression they knew was this preparation of graves.

There they were, the four markers of her four Companions, the founders of GOB and the new world she alone had survived to see. Religion, they decided, the bonding of religion, its stricture against murder, must be the cornerstone. But what religion? One without gods; but how could that be religion, how could that become a popular religion? People had always needed icons, idols.

'We could make each person their own idol, so to speak,' Clare had been the first to suggest. 'Not a cult of the self. Nothing to do with that,' she added hastily. 'But each person as god in the way that people hold in common,' she stumbled as they all looked on, suspicious and confused. 'The body,' she finished, with a little flourish in her tremulous voice. 'The gods of the body.'

'Against whom,' Curie followed the thought to its logical conclusion, 'the one unforgivable sin is murder, or destruction in any form.'

'Abortion?' Davy challenged.

They almost smiled at the grotesque joke of it. Abortion! When there existed so few of the bodies they were planning to deify. It was easy to see them as gods, the remnant that remained. They had the sadness of deities who had outlived their time.

'All right,' Davy growled, 'Maybe it's not an issue yet.'

They would have to establish a school for the continued study of the cult itself, to keep it elastic, to guard against it becoming fossilized or nostalgic. Above all, they had to keep their own nostalgia at bay, to avoid contaminating the new religion with it. In the end, it had had more to do with the body cults of the late twentieth century than with Judeo-Christianity. They had sought to harness the narcissism which had inspired such intense discipline. They turned it outward, to socialize it, and profoundly inward, to spiritualize it, as well. There were practical implications. Theology and anatomy were linked as never before. It was necessary that each person be a healer, a priest, a world unto herself, equally necessary that their vision be thoroughly communal. As theirs had been, finally, the vision of the four unlikely founders.

Four? She frowned down at the little row of graves at her feet, sat herself down on the grass in front of them. Five. Why had she left herself out of the count? She was cut off from them now, no less than from the children who were off preparing themselves for their festival, with all the seriousness of children getting ready to perform for their elders. She was the elder they performed for. Who would be the adult when she was gone?

Definitions have changed, she argued, as if with the four of them. Adult means something different now. There is no sophistication in the old sense.

No maturity either, came the answering argument.

She patted India's little mound as she had once patted the pregnant mound of her stomach. Pregnant now with grubby underground life. At least the life of the underneath had returned, worms did their eternal stretching as if from sleep, once again. They, too, had become rare and therefore beautiful.

They always were, she contradicted herself. We were spoiled, and we forgot. Spoiled by the excess that bubbled over in the rain, the twisting worms we used to step on without compunction. After all, they could live on, broken in two. They had lost that capacity now. Why did that seem such a terrible loss, so terrible that her tears spilled on India's ground?

Next was Ruth's. There on the top, tangled in the grass, visible to her eyes alone, was the key to the church they had all lived in together, so incalculably long ago. Ruth had carried it through everything. Curie had seen her bite down on it in agony, like an epileptic biting on a spoon. She had carried it in her mouth sometimes, as they moved in their long march, sometimes on all fours. It seemed to calm and contain her, like a bit in a horse's mouth.

Clare. One of her own tiny sculptures was curled in the grass, a zebra with tiny stripes, curled in a shy half-moon of drowsy peacefulness. Curie picked it up and fondled it, careful not to chip the delicate thing. Time had whittled it down, made it finer, but not yet crumbled it.

Davy, like India, had kept nothing, but Curie had worked her little plot into the rough outline of a foot, green as the bronze charioteer's she remembered from the museum at Delphi, the most perfect feet in the world; except for Davy's. Even the absurd grass foot could summon a sense of Davy's tiny little hands and feet, set incongruously on her tough frame. But the toughness was deliberate, a second nature rather than a first.

'What're you doing here,' she'd complain, if she could, 'mooning over my poor little pickled feet?'

She'd say I only ever did like them because they made me feel strong, Curie remembered ruefully. Davy saw the megalomaniac in the making, if anyone did. Maybe that was why she turned to Clare, poor confused Clare, a crazed and accidental prophet. But she had fulfilled her destiny and achieved her dignity at last. She worked in clay, finally. Her creativity flowered in the one medium that remained, designing both real, remembered creatures and fantastic, invented ones. She decided on her deathbed that they would do only harm in the new world, only promote morbid curiosity and wistfulness.

'Destroy them,' she'd made them promise. 'Break them up and bury them with me.'

India, tight-lipped, had carried out her wishes to the letter. But Curie had made off with the little zebra, which she meant to preserve at least for the duration of her own lifetime.

One of the Potters stood watching her, leaning on a rake. She turned and began nonchalantly to tidy her own grave. It was customary that each person worked alone in the Field unless she brought someone along as a ritual, to

31

underline a friendship. You learned a lot about someone from her grave.

The Potter came over, no doubt to learn about her from hers. She examined the little triangle with a critical eye. It was a bit neglected, and that wouldn't do.

'You have too many duties to be assiduous here, M-other,' the Potter addressed her.

'There's no excuse,' she said firmly. 'For me or anyone else. But it looks a little neater than I had any right to expect, in fact they all, all my –'

She stopped. All my graves, she had been about to say.

'I give them a little brush-up now and then,' he said gently.

At least, she thought he was he. You'd have to lie underneath him like a car and peer up, to be sure, and even then you might not know. The Potters were mutants. They were all mutants, but the Potters were variants even among themselves. No two looked alike. How, she frowned, had they come to care for the Field as a tribal task? She looked around suddenly, another question on the heels of that one.

'Where are the Potters' graves?' she asked him timidly. 'Don't you –'

'Oh, yes, we make them,' he assured her. 'We follow a somewhat adapted version of the Gods of the Body,' he said with what could have been a sardonic smile.

Curie never felt sure of where she was with the Potters. They were a bit shadowy, though substantial enough, tough in fact, much tougher than the M-others of GOB. Did they consider their role inferior, she wondered; but there were no concepts for such things.

'There,' he was gesturing, 'And there, and there.'

'But they're all the same!'

He nodded. 'You must allow us our heresy, M-other. We are so different in life, we prefer to be uniform in death.'

No wonder they worked so hard. The patches he had

pointed out to her were so utterly alike that the Field turned into a giant mirror under her gaze. She had taken it for lawn before, not for graves. Did he realize, this subtly subversive creature, that she immediately wondered why she, Curie, Professor of the GOB Sem, had not been consulted before they went ahead and dug their uniform graves?

No, she was glad they hadn't come for permission. She might have refused them. The sight of all those identical mounds, now that she knew what they were, filled her with shaking. They were too much like other graves in other times, much too much. She walked away from the Potter, with an inclination he returned. When she half-turned around she saw that he was kneeling down to pare Davy's blue-green foot.

How dare he! She felt doubly violated. First they went ahead and simply did as they wished with their graves, going right against the custom. Then he came and pottered round her friends' last symbols. No. She stopped herself and sat down wearily on, she supposed spitefully, a Potter's grave; her own last personal symbols. The triangle that her grave was carved into, well, yes, that stood for the mess she and Davy and Clare had got themselves into, and it stood, ironically, as a religious sign as well. But it meant little to her, her own plot. Only her friends'.

So she was the heretic. She broke the custom far more seriously than the Potters, by not caring. It was clear that they cared, clear by the lengths they went to to make their graves reflect each others'. It seemed odd of them to leave their secret unconfessed, so that the M-others unconsciously walked, sat, played and picnicked on their plots. It seemed a perverse sort of martyrdom, when all they needed do to prevent it was announce what those little patches of moss and fern and palm actually were. Their graves.

They used the same tone Sophia had taken in the classroom earlier, when they said 'M-other', the Potters.

And yet it was their choice not to share the title. There was an irony, a mockery there. Irony and mockery were not part of GOB. They were moods of speech too subtle and sophisticated for the M-others, but not for Sophia. Had she first experienced them here, with the Potters? There was no non-sororization rule. Curie almost choked on her thoughts. There was simply a natural division, she had thought, or been about to think. How, when, had her unconscious racism developed, how had she let it develop? Had it spread?

Maybe that was the reason for the Potter's sardonic look. Sophia could hardly claim that there was any discrimination practised in GOB against her, Curie argued with herself, and then argued back: oh, yes, she could. As heir apparent to Curie, she could well argue that her right to a questioning, a questing intelligence was interfered with.

She was meant to develop all the incisive skills and then hold back from using them. It was true. The unspoken limitations placed on a successor would hardly trouble any of the others. They had more basic limitations. But Sophia was different.

So she has something in common with the Potters, so she has made contact with them, Curie dreamed to herself, sitting in the smoky twilight air of the Field. Just what I would do in her place. Just as I would track me, Curie, the one with all the secrets, would give me no rest until I told.

I don't even have to go to bed with her. She has entered me, come right into me. She's here. Like a child I carry. A daughter. Because we are alike, or at least I assume that, I identify. I feel or make a likeness between us. This has not happened to me in fifty years of life.

Tears fell on her face. The imprint on her cheeks felt sharp, gouging, like ice breaking up. Her tears had been impersonal, for fifty years. They had been shed for other people, most of them here in this very field. But these tears were for herself, and she despised them.

Maybe I'll appoint one of them, she thought, making her mind swerve from this abrupt excess of emotion to her – its, anyway – rightful preoccupations. A Potter. That would solve the schism between the two worlds. It would strengthen the M-others to learn a little sarcasm and scepticism. She remembered the intensity with which some of them had embraced her lecture of the morning, the uncritical intensity. The Founding Mothers had anticipated an intense need for religion. That was the premise on which the Gods of the Body was built. But surely that was enough? A virtual theocracy with a Seminary which all attended, where theology was once again the Queen of Sciences, the only science.

If more was needed, it must be a secular more. They had gone as far as they could with religion. Hence the advantage of a Potter as Professor. She sensed a quiet agnosticism, tinged with some kind of mystical awareness; perhaps? The phrases slipped and shrieked, too clumsy, too solid. The Field was a fluid sort of place, and the Potters, making it a looking glass of sorts, had shown themselves capable of originality and humour.

I'll decide tonight, she decided. Whatever happens, I will announce my retirement and my successor at dawn. I can't pretend to know any more answers. I can't even be bothered to make up any more, she yawned. How good it will be to come to festivals like this as a spectator.

She watched the Potters. Some of them moved oddly. They scuttered round the field, hunched like the old she had thought of as she set out. Maybe it was thought that kept them doubled over, too; or laughter, of course. Somehow that was a more uncomfortable thought. They lived close to the earth, and to death, there was no doubt of that. There were rumours that they communicated with the dead. They handled the graves gently, held the flowers like homunculi, between careful hands. Like midwives to the dead, she thought idly. Each planting was a kind of

35

resurrection. That, too, was theory to her, dry and repetitive as the 'blue' routine. But to them, she saw, startled, it was real. They moved like alchemists. Somehow they even looked tall as they lumbered among the graves, which they were not. They were short and squat, but they moved as if tall, they moved, she thought, like trees. They moved in a strange, stately dance, the way trees would dance.

She put her head in her hands again. Madness certainly spread fast, once it started. The Potters were dancing trees now, Sophia a spy in conspiracy with them – or was Sophia only a figment of her overheated imagination? Did Sophia exist at all, other than as a split-off fragment of conscience come to warn her, or a demon come to tempt?

Enough! 'Enough' had become her mantra. She felt revulsion for the Field today, she realized. She felt it had failed totally in its purpose. They hadn't made death more tolerable or brought it closer to integration with life, so that life wouldn't be hedged or foreshortened by its anonymous shadow. They'd simply made it into a fairy tale illustrated by sweet little child-pictures from the sweet little child M-others. Their graves were games.

The Potters' graves had far more elegance. She got up and walked again. The Potters' graves had restraint and dignity. The M-others' were just dollhouses, window boxes. It was like the stork bringing babies, the notion that these kitschy plots could contain death. Death would leer and laugh a ribald laugh here, were it not for the Potters.

But what was wrong with it, she wondered, staring. Why was it a travesty of their original aim? Something had eluded them. The little kindergarten efforts were touchingly insufficient. They became frightening when you realized that that was all there was, the sum total of individual expression in GOB.

Maybe I think this simply because I'm old, she comforted herself, getting up slowly, feeling gravity tugging her joints as if calling her down with the others. My view of things is shrunken and jaundiced and weak, like my body. It isn't what's outside me that's insufficient, it's what's inside. It's my inner world that's rotting, becoming a travesty of the original aim.

She walked stiffly down to the site of the festival. The Potters had piled branches high for fires, piled them in clearings she now recognized as graves. She frowned, deeply troubled to think they sacrificed their own holy ground to the yearly fertility rite. The one she'd talked to came up and offered her a glass of palm wine, which she accepted gratefully, thinking, waiters and caterers they are, and caretakers to boot. How could this happen?

'Tell me,' she asked him gently, sipping from the glass after she had lifted it to him, which he acknowledged with a sober dip of his whiskery little face, 'Don't you mind, giving up your – space – to the festival?'

She was on treacherous ground herself. She had almost said 'to our festival' –

'But it is our festival too,' he said simply. 'And you see, M-other, so many of us die.'

She looked around her once more. Of course, they must. Every spare inch of ground was planted in that distinctive way that she could now identify.

'Have you always –' she asked helplessly. Their grief-load was so much greater. And they had never said. That might even be why they left their graves so plain, so the numbers would not be so conspicuous, so shocking. But whom were they sparing?

He nodded, 'Always, some by accident – we have many stillbirths.'

Some by accident? She turned to question him further, to find him gone from her elbow. What was he insinuating? That they practised some kind of ritual killing was too remote a possibility to entertain. But that they, as a mutated species, did away with the most painfully twisted and deformed of their offspring – was that the burden of his observation?

37

And once again, they hadn't asked. They had simply acted as they chose to act, as they thought best. Anarchically, within the tightly-knit GOB. How could she deal with it? How could she not? To leave it hanging for her successor to discover and attempt to correct, if there was a corrective, if –

It amounted to a schism. The Potters were the gravediggers and distillers of GOB. Like Davy, she thought fondly, but it was a dark smile that spread as she sat down, gripping her glass tightly. Davy had made the first intoxicants in the new world, after they'd decided to allow such things if they could locate their makings and mixings.

'I'll find them, if there are any to be found,' Davy had muttered, and gone in search of the remaining leaf, stem or blade that could be fermented to produce alcohol, or facsimile thereof.

'In a cult of the body,' Ruth had objected, at the start, 'surely we don't want to legitimize poisons?'

'But people have always needed some kind of instant transforming elixir,' said Davy, ostentatiously for her. She kept her speech direct and simple, ordinarily. 'I think it's a valid, authentic need.'

'She's taking the piss,' Clare sang, interpreting Davy as once she would not have dared to do in Curie's presence. 'She just wants to get pissed.'

'Right!' Davy confirmed.

Ruth had sighed consent. India was cautiously pro-stimulant, Clare was wryly enthusiastic. Wryness was a feature of her old age. Curie was in favour of the hunt for stimulants, undignified and inappropriate as it might be. For all their sakes, she felt, it was worth a try. They needed something, and if that was not what they needed, it had served as an efficient enough substitute before.

A chant began far off. The cult of the Heart would begin the festival. Their particular ballet would be lurid and loud.

38

Each cult had developed its own separate style and its own routines, like folk dances. They taught the simple, unsubtle steps to new recruits. It was a tradition of sorts.

The costumes, too, had become stylized. They had taken their stamp from the spectrum of the body's own shades. Also, perhaps, Curie mused, from the Founding Mothers' own inherited tastes. If Ruth was their heart, in the old days, her children, the Hearts, wore purple, one of her own passionate preferences.

Suddenly Curie was swept backwards by a wave of memory. Davy had perfected the magical formula for forgetfulness, or was it for remembering? For judicious selection, perhaps – at any rate, she had found it. They were about to celebrate her discovery, and her very survival. They had feared for her life as she brewed and tasted and swore, surrounded by miniature trees in earthenware pots. The five species had not yet grown back. All that grew were myriad dwarves, perfect bonsai trees, as if in commemoration of those who had first felt the flaying blast. By the time she succeeded in her quest for an elixir, less of youth than of agelessness, the little trees she had milked were withered and stooped, and would not be revived.

Ruth had worn purple that night. Ruth had become uncharacteristically bombed. Curie shuddered at the old slang term. They had remembered it that night, had used it swaggeringly, mockingly, then helplessly, in alcoholic regression, as their fierce inhibitions gave way to fiercer grief and then to the fierce exorcism of passion. There was only one exception, one exclusion, one of the five who clung to inhibition.

'Bombed,' she heard the old, beloved voices sing hysterically as the Hearts approached, storming and stamping through the blue haze of early night. 'We're bombed all right,' the voices sang on, healing fury in their chant. It was ironic to think that shortly thereafter they had begun to die.

39

She turned away from the thought. Not another irony, not this one that twisted and pulled at her own heart while the rowdy devotees of the Heart (What did they know of it? Less than of death, or as little, at least, and that, too, was her doing.) clambered into position in front of her.

Their long cloaks glittered with sequins like bits of mica. Each one was a separate stained-glass window as they changed their tread and strode solemnly before her. The cloaks were scarlet and the suits they wore underneath all-in-ones, – like babies' rompers, she always thought unfairly – were deep blue. When they moved, they made purple slashes in the darkness.

Sophia came and sat down next to her with a bump, as though she were slightly drunk. If she hobnobbed with the Potters, of course, she might have open access to the palm wine. Curie felt a clutch of concern, both anguished and angry. Memory had taken her back to that other festival. Could it be for a reason, was this a parallel? Were the M-others about to begin their decline as the mothers, *their* mothers, had done? Was Sophia about to die?

Stop it, she told herself sharply. The parallels are of your own making. She accepted another glass of wine from a discreetly hovering Potter, and noted that Sophia did the same, with avidity. Let this night be a parallel to the other for me, only for me, she prayed. I am alone now, as then. Let it bring my death in its wake, she prayed to the Four Companions, as that other night brought yours.

The Hearts had stepped up their tempo again. They looked less like stained-glass windows now and more like giant playing cards from a strange, repetitive deck. The wine worked in her, and she wanted to put her head on Sophia's shoulder and weep. To whom could she say what was in her mind, what image or memory could she share? Her reflections of the afternoon came back to her, no longer abstract but animate. How was life possible without some prospect of sharing, even if that prospect was illusion?

40

Maybe life was impossible without illusion. She had tried to live on in unflinching clarity. Now she flinched, and was not even clear.

Sophia put an arm around her as though she sensed the inward cringing. Or had she so lost control as to make an involuntary movement?

'They're beautiful,' Sophia murmured as if in dreamy agreement.

Curie could only nod in the darkness. So much for illusion. Sophia thought she had shivered with the thrill of the spectacle, and she could not say otherwise, could not contradict her misapprehension. She would not be understood. She could not be understood. Usually she accepted it, resignedly, as she had accepted the wine, as she now accepted more. Tonight memory had undermined her acceptance. Tonight she could hardly choke back the meaningless words. 'Look,' she wanted to cry, 'They're just like the pack of cards in Alice – remember? Remember?'

But Sophia was asking her an improper question. Sophia was asking her whether she had ever gone down with a Heart, and Sophia was giggling in the darkness as she asked.

Curie tried to recover a semblance of authoritative gravity. But her emotions were ready for any expression. Denied sorrow or anger, they sped to seize giddiness and girlish laughter. She heard an undignified snort, and her hand came up to cover her mouth as she realized its source.

Sophia's hand came up in turn, and pulled hers away. 'Confess,' she whispered, and giggled again. 'Come on, Curie. Did you, ever?'

Curie shook her head, as stiffly as she could manage. 'They were never really my suit,' she heard herself say in a thin, laughing voice, then snorted again, at her private pun. 'I mean they never really suited me,' she reiterated, laughing again. It had to stop. The boiling tears were pressed too close behind. They would explode like a geyser.

'You mean you never gave them a chance,' Sophia teased. 'Such prejudice, M-other. I did,' she confided, moving closer. 'And I can tell you on authority, you were right.'

On authority, Curie thought groggily, what does she mean? How did she get hold of the notion of testing and trying, of doing research? It was not a medieval idea. And they lived in a medieval world.

Then she was swept up into the dance. The Hearts swirled a heavy cape around her shoulders, and planted her in their circle. There was fire blazing at the centre, placed, she supposed, by the Potters. Heat, smoke and light all seemed part of the pounding dance. The rhythm quickened without lightening. Heaviness was a hallmark of the Hearts. Was that Sophia's scientifically arrived-at objection, she wondered. Another sort of fire made her wish she could take off the cloak as the rest of the circle were doing, with great flashing and swishing of cloth, like toreadors. But it was her place to remain robed while the others were naked.

I am the bull, she thought gloomily. She felt dark and sullen and furious. The other, inward fire that gnawed at her so painfully was jealousy.

She was lifted onto a broad pair of shoulders, solid as a throne. She looked out proudly, an earthbound bull no more, only to see Sophia standing in animated conversation with a cluster of Potters at the furthest edge of the verge.

She was swung onto another pair of shoulders, and another, while jealous rage bellowed inside her. Sophia was not even paying attention, as she, Curie, was ceremoniously passed round the circle. *Not even paying attention. To me*, Curie, in my moment of triumph, roaring like a minotaur with a toothache. Except that for some strange reason there were no more toothaches. Just as there were no more toothbrushes or toothpaste, no more need. Teeth were uniformly yellow, like dogs'.

Just as there was meant to be no more jealousy. She

thudded gracelessly onto another shoulder, her eyes misted with tears. If she didn't pay attention, she'd land ignominiously in the grass, or the flames. She'd be burnt as a witch after all. Serve her right for blubbing because she didn't have a toothbrush. Or was she snivelling over the equally archaic emotion she'd discovered she did have?

No matter. She winked away the tears. She was the Queen of Hearts, now. The rhythm slowed. The air hummed, vibrated. The Hearts themselves vibrated like tuning forks, glistening with sweat. Bare forked animals. Her mind winked with quotations like neon, old neon signs with letters missing, with words missing, with meaning missing. No matter.

> Now, no matter, child, the name
> Sorrow's springs are the same

The lines winked off and on relentlessly. She was gently shouldered around once more, the last lap. Then there would be blessed quiet, after the raucous Hearts had done.

> The Queen of Hearts
> She had some tarts

After the raucous heart that thudded and kicked like a quickening child inside her. How did she know what a child felt like? Although she was a mother, many times over.

> Now no matter

She was grounded again, and glad to be. Now she could wait patiently for the tuning forks to still, for the final calm.

> child the name

Then a massage before the next cult appeared. She needed it, the quiet and the massage. But the humming went on, grew denser. The rhythm quickened again, moving towards their original thumping, pumping beat.

> Sorrow's springs

Were they giving themselves an encore? Imaginations might not grow in GOB, but egos did. She would have to make a rule against repetition at the festival. She would have to advise her successor to so do.

43

are the same

But this was no mere encore. Something new was happening. She was picked up and carried horizontally, face up to the handful of rather dusty stars that was still visible. She was too stunned to protest or even to speak, and too interested, as she had been too interested in the Potter, that afternoon, to rebuke him for his revelations. This was a revelation. She would rebuke them afterwards.

The Hearts had formed two lines, one on either side of her. Their right hands locked beneath her. Their left hands, she felt rather than saw, wound through the air in a rowing sort of motion. Very much a rowing sort of motion, though they couldn't know that. They were just batting the air with their hands, unconsciously imitating something real, like children. Or perhaps the action of rowing was an imitation of childlike wind-batting, perhaps all machines imitated primitive human movements and gestures. What could it matter now, when machines were no more? She sighed and closed her eyes.

She was both boat and passenger. They were galley slaves and mariners. She was passive, they active, as they laboured to carry her on their human litter. There was nothing menial in their attitude as they ferried her – to where?

To the river. She had forgotten to bring the river into her morning homily. She sighed again. Let them be aware that her memory was going, then. It would justify her departure. Little wonder her memory frayed, the way she had suppressed and savaged it.

The river. She faced it with affection. Sweet brown water, charcoal now. They waited patiently, as if to assure themselves that they had her full attention, as if they sensed she was in reverie, induced by the slow movement of the water, by its very smell. Water smelled sourer than it had before, and its taste was bitter. But something of the original, curiously strong tang had come back after an initial period of foulness. She had found that one of the worst trials, the sick stench of the undrinkable water.

She was lifted up and over the grassy bank. For a wild second she believed they were going to heave her into the dense, snaking mass of the river, feed her to it. Her witch-trial would be ordeal by water, a ducking.

But there was no splash, no wetness. Only wood and movement. She was in a boat. There were no boats. There was no notion of navigation. There was no need of either.

It was a dream. But how wonderful, to be in motion again on the water, how she had missed it! Self-locomotion was the rule for GOB. They had laid that down as an absolute. Trouble had come with the sound of a motor, the need for oil and rubber and tons of water. Death had come to so many, from their cars and their planes; and their boats.

But not from the humble rowboat, she argued with the five of them, her younger self included, the Moses-women.

But it will never stop there, they argued back, including her young, rigid, resolute self.

The Hearts sang as they rowed her, and all the M-others – for all she knew, the Potters, too – sang with them, from the shore. The song on the water and the song on the shore chased each other, slightly out of time, making an echo. The song was heavy and stern, an uncanny echo, in itself, of the Volga Boat Song. It left her defence-less, without distractions. The combination of the heavily reminiscent music and the sensation of being in a boat again – that *again* thundered in her – broke through the monotonous cadence the stray verses had set up in her mind, scattered her random meditations on the nature of machines, the reasoning behind their proscription.

She began to hear the words. They were sad, full of reflections on the final crossings of the water, on the different levels of travel. No journey was without risk and resonance of birth and death. She was shocked into listen-ing, now, more jolted by their lyrics than by the fact of the

45

rowboat itself. It might have been a toy. She could allow them a toy. But they made the link beween death and all human departures, between birth and all arrivals. How had they done that? What did they know of farewells, when they lived huddled together?

> 'Parting is all we know of ever
> And all we need of never –'

She was bolt upright now, on the rough little seat, confused and stricken. How had they come upon that tall sentiment in their shrunken souls? Was it just a case of monkeys with typewriters – not that they had typewriters! – would they, next year or the year after, correct the lines and unknowingly salute Emily Dickinson with the verbatim text?

> 'Parting is all we know of heaven
> And all we need of hell –'

Heaven and hell meant nothing to them, or so she thought. Unless they, too, were constructs of the psyche which would surface in time, infallibly, just as, it seemed, boats would surface on water. It was all impossible, it was all a dream, the forbidden first machine, the leap of imagination, linking locomotion with human life. Both were leaps of the imagination, the second, to her mind, the greater leap, ideas like aerialists linking in mid-air. But they had no imaginations! Or so she had believed.

They sang more softly now, bringing her back to the throng on the riverside. She must decide what to do. A spontaneous gesture of some sort was called for, but what? Anger or condescension? Her thoughts wound furiously, but led nowhere. She realized how they had made the leap as she was handed off the boat. It was the Heart itself, the organ they served, that had led them to this. The Diastole-systole, for which they knew only much simpler words, was the cadence of rowing itself, the rhythm that carried the blood, that moved the organism. They had worked it out from that. And then, her thoughts raced on, on another level, too, it was the heart that had taught them the

46

metaphor of travel and death, of travel and birth. The five Moses-women had had too little faith in the resources of the body, in its creativity.

There was no pause in the proceedings. She was gently guided rather than carried this time, led like a blind woman back to the fire. Her teeth were chattering. A few Potters had stayed to tend it. Her clothing was gently removed and her massage began, to the Boat Song hummed in a low, throaty tone.

She tensed. Her lips set. They had not come running to her with their discovery, oh, no! They had saved it, shrouded it in secrecy, deceived her. Candour was gone from the Body, and deceit installed in its place. That would be the theme of her remarks, when she was given an opportunity to make them. She trembled with anger, then closed her eyes and forced herself to breathe in harmony with the massaging fingers. She must maintain control now, at all costs. Make a dignified end. She was still determined to choose her successor that very night, despite the disruption. Her mind went again to the Potters.

Heretics. They had made secret decisions and choices. They knew the little death in every choice. Something was left out to die, every time you decided, some fragment of being, of self, potential or actual. They had learned to live with that, and communicated it, it would appear, to the M-others. The choice, the political choice of a new leader, had already been made, or at least indicated.

A Potter waited with her refilled glass, handed it to her as she sat up. Sophia waited, too. In the end the massage had been irresistible and her body throbbed with satisfaction like the contractions of the womb after orgasm. That, too, was like the reverberations of love for the dead, she thought sadly as she sipped from her glass – a throbbing, an echo that established what had been, the moment of closeness, of completeness that was no more. And then the sadness, like the sadness that afflicted her now.

Sophia took her hand and flexed it gently.

'You look so lonely, Curie, so apart.'

'I am apart,' she said steadily.

'You are a part,' the Potter said in a gutteral voice.

Curie looked at him sidewise. Word-games, too? She wondered whether – he? – had been Sophia's massage partner, for all took part in the ritual massage. She was almost amused by the stab of jealousy that visited her at the thought. It seemed so frivolous now.

Then her attention was distracted. The Hands and Arms were on their way, bells jingling as they approached, turning cartwheels, pausing to balance themselves in perfect handstands. She sat up straighter, in anticipation. If she had favourites, they were the Hands. She would forget all the nonsense and nostalgia and settle into the festival now. It was only a hiccup, after all.

Everything she loved in life was a task of the hands, or a delight of the hands, everything that gave her joy. Cooking, planting, praying, writing, even love. Cat's cradles, church steeples, could all be crafted by the hands. What was speech of the lips only, without the illustration of the hands?

With them, running behind, came the Feet, the babies of the body. If the hands were its prodigies, the feet were its clowns, its holy fools, wriggly and silly and utterly serious. They were universal pets. They had poignancy, orphaned at the extremity of the body, far from the brain, often out in the cold. But they were cheerful and fertile, with their two sets of quintuplet toes, the plump, cherubic babies' babies.

The Hands divested themselves of their tinkling bells. They stood in formation. They sang, another travellers' song, remembering their companions in the graveyard, those who had travelled beyond them. The simple words stung.

The Feet were the accompaniment, thumping a rhythm,

48

and then a tune rose from them and the Hands fell silent. The last lines of their song had begged a blessing from the friends they recalled and honoured. She joined in the plea with impulsive fervour.

But now the song changed. The Hands were background music, whirling round, round, not like the rowers but like something she could not quite name, as they hummed a deep counterpoint to the tune of the Feet, another sound reminiscent, but of what? She could not place it.

The sound grew stronger, the words louder. It described the thing she was looking for, the thing that had no name. It was wind-borne, the words claimed, borne by the wind and born of the wind. Then it described the process of its birth in crystal-clear language, language so pure and accurate it was both poetry and science. The song described the displacement of wind which in turn held up the displacing wing (for wing it was, although there were no birds to give them such a vision), just as the water displaced by the boat supported it in turn. Both wind and water were able to mother wind and water-wings because of their own greater volume.

Curie was stupefied. Together the Hands and the Feet formed the shape of a bird, a huge bird with a dropped beak. Once again she was lifted and placed inside the configuration they made. She looked out and down – out of what? down from what? – and saw Sophia and the Potter wave to her from the ground. She was airborne, she was flying, for the first time in her life she was aboard the drop-beaked giant, Concorde.

We will walk as the wind walks, the song went on. We will climb to the canopy and beyond, to the sky. Someday. The Arms lifted her like a child, threw her and caught her again. So a child first dreams of flight, first conceives of it. They were straining to explain their strange ambition to her, to translate their dream. She wept as she was tossed and thrown again, the song billowing around her. She had bound their feet, as surely as if she had actually hobbled them with splints and bandages. She could not bind their dreams.

She wept less for her own guilt than for their innocence as they tried so hard to describe what she alone, of all of them, had seen and known, tried with the inadequate tools she had given them. Only Sophia, and the Potter behind her, turned accusing eyes upwards as she landed, all smiles, to show how much she had enjoyed her flight, more to thank them for their effort of communication. They were the ringleaders, those two.

The ringleaders indicated that they would together administer her next massage. She wanted to protest but was reluctant to create any further disruption, and anyway, she couldn't trust her voice. She lay down obediently and felt Sophia's hand rove over her skin, less giving a massage than taking a reading of some sort, while the Potter massaged as if he had a million attachments, with brushlike and sucker-like movements and currents. Sophia's hands were half-dutiful, half-angry. The Potter's were skilful and neutral. They made her feel like a car being washed.

The massage was mercifully short. She was handed a drink, fruit juice this time, to rest and refresh the body between bouts of wine. She downed it and her glass was refilled with wine, which she gratefully sipped. The Brains would be next. She dreaded their contribution, their revelation. Even under normal circumstances she found them a bit of a trial.

The cult of the Brain included the smaller groups devoted to the eyes, ears, mouth, and nose. All the major cults had their offshoots. People could worship anything. Everything held the combination of eroticism and aestheticism that worship required, plus the pinch of mystery. Toenails, necks, elbows, all had their disciples. Wisdom was equally promiscuous. It could be cultivated anywhere. It was implicit in rapt contemplation and study. Only the attitude mattered, the concentration. Not the object.

Sophia placed a kiss on her neck as if she were planting a seed. The Potter looked on. There was neither envy nor voyeurism in his glance, only interest. Curie looked away resentfully. The Potters seemed to challenge her without a word, to question not so much her authority as the superiority on which it rested.

The Brains marched like soldiers, or chessmen. They wore shining reflectors on their foreheads, like the doctors of another time. A high forehead was considered by them to be a mark of great favour, not surprisingly. The Potters had uniformly low foreheads. She glanced at the Potter beside her and thought that he was smiling in a caustic sort of way at the advancing ranks of Brains in white togas with silver reflectors. At least his smile seemed caustic. It was hard to read. Perhaps the Potters felt the Brains looked down on them for their foreheads? Did they? Did she?

She looked around, blinking in the dark. What would the reflectors reflect? Would they reinvent the wheel? It seemed a logical guess, she thought smugly, then shook her head at herself. She must pay attention. But the notion of flight, she thought dreamily, mesmerized by the traditional geometric dance the Brains performed, must have come in part from the wafting grass skirts the Hands and Feet wore, from the wind-chime jewellery they loved.

The next thing she knew, a circle of Brains had come to stand around her and Sophia and the Potter. They stared intently at the Potter, almost glared, and he stared coolly, intently back. Then a signal passed, like a handshake, though it wasn't, and the Potter stood up as one Brain separated herself out from the rest to confront him.

Are they going to fight, she wondered. She was frightened. Anything could happen tonight. The festival would be ruined, GOB degraded, if they fought. But how could she interfere?

Besides, interference might be ineffectual, further

undermining her control. She could not afford to risk that, not now. She would have to sit tight and watch. The Potter turned abruptly and shot her an ironic glance, as if he knew why she sat silent. Then he turned back to the Brain, and the atmosphere of intense concentration between them deepened and spread. She could feel herself being gathered into the glance that went between them, as if the force of their two expressions, trained on each other, was a construction, a suspension bridge on which she stood, and not alone. She sensed that the rest of GOB stood on that bridge with her, agorophobic and claustrophobic at once, crammed into so small and intimate a space as the distance between two faces that burned their gazes into one another. Small and intimate, the space, and vast, impersonal, swept with howling winds. The Potter and the Brain were almost two separate institutions, as they demonstrated their formal willingness to rendezvous, and stiffened with their private fear.

Never had she felt so caught in the cross-fire between two others, or so excluded. Never, unless long ago with Davy and Clare – but she put the thought from her. She was here. She was a captive audience as a child is a captive audience and also, in fact or fantasy, a participant in the rows and reconciliations of its parents.

Then she laughed, and was jostled by the laughter of those around her. Why should she laugh, why should they? Because there had been a joke, she had heard it with her own ears, as children used to say. Then again, had her ears been the receptors? There had been a joke and she had taken it in and laughed. It had passed between the Potter and the Brain and broken their tension as well as everyone else's. But who had told it? How had she heard it, or overheard it?

There was silence again as the two gazes locked anew. But the general laughter had left a buzz of commotion and distraction in the air, and the bridge would not link up. It

52

had been taut as steel before. Now there was slackness and release in the air.

The Potter and the Brain each took a step forward, embraced each other and began to dance. Curie was grabbed and pirouetted on Sophia's arm. Who's leading, she wanted to ask indignantly, but dared not. She was following. That much was certain.

She had witnessed, no, she had participated in, a demonstration of telepathy. In fact, she felt uneasily certain that it was her resistance, her questions, that had led to the breakdown of contact. Whatever the truth of that conjecture (which might derive from her wish to retain control, after all), the demonstration had been awesome.

She was pushed brusquely into the grass for another massage. Again it was Sophia and the Potter who tackled her. She felt the tremor in him, after his exertions.

'Next time will be longer,' he said cheerfully. 'This was good for the first mass attempt. We have much more success with individuals, M-other.'

She nodded and burrowed further down into the grass. Every fibre of her screamed interrogation at him. Where had these individual successes occurred? In the Field no doubt, on the Potters' secret graves. Secrets on secrets on secrets. But she would bide her time, she would safeguard her dignity. Besides, she was frightened. She burrowed down to escape from whatever powers her masseur might possess. What if he could read her mind?

The massage stopped as if on cue. She turned to look at him, determined to have the truth, but her gaze was arrested as the Genital cults arrived in their splendid, glistening nakedness, wearing only hats or anklets or wristbands that suggested genital textures and hues. They were followed by the Anal Apostles, a jolly little band, almost as popular as the Feet and Toes. They were whimsically aware of the absurdity and sensitivity of their chosen site. That the last act of life was the act of defecation did not escape them, neither the bull's-eye nature of the asshole as sexual target. Its prominence in both sex and death gave to these prime and essential aspects of human life a grotesque and clownish element was both their pride and their humility.

The Vaginalics and Phallics, the Fallopes, the Labyrinthics, as the womb-cult somewhat pretentiously called itself, the Testiculars, also a rather sticky bunch, or so Curie thought, began their sinuous, seductive interweavings around the fire. She groaned to herself as she tried to imagine what their interpolation would incorporate into the Body. Had they synthesized DNA perhaps, or produced a test-tube M-other for her delectation and delight? Or a Potter, complete with defects? That *would* be a feat.

A glass was at her elbow. *The* Potter, Sophia's Potter, held it. There was no mistaking the look of distaste on his face, which comprehended and disdained her sarcasm in one expressive glance, as he filled the glass she had rapidly emptied.

Serves you right, you nosy hermaphrodite, she thought; but he appeared to be gone. She turned her attention back to the Genitals. They did the dance of the sperm and the dance of the egg. It was all traditional so far. The desperation of the sperm was both pitiful and farcical. The untouched egg crumbled and flowed away. Curie yawned. This part was always long-winded, till fertilization occurred.

At last, she thought crossly, now they can get on with it. A bottle appeared at her elbow and filled her glass again as a hoot of laughter rang in her ear. It was the Potter. He shook his head at her, and wandered off like a wine waiter, into the crowd.

At least he doesn't hold grudges, she reasoned. Maybe if you're telepathic you can't afford to. His interruption had spared her the excitement of implantation, and taken her through to the embryo. Then a lissome Vaginalic began to dance alongside the group, hissing and darting her tongue out as she twisted and slid over and under the others.

54

She was there every year. This was no departure. But Curie felt as if she had never really seen her before, or seen what she stood for. How did she get there? There were no snakes in GOB. Where did she come from, if not from the same place the boat and the plane and their ability to meet had come from? She had not taught them the snake, either.

They danced together. There was no enmity between them. The snake enclosed the embryo in a protective embrace, then stretched lengthwise to become the umbilicus. When it was cut, it became the tongue.

It would take a jealous god to introduce fear of the snake into GOB. Or goddess. She had denied them knowledge of good and evil, she had been that miserly deity. But she had failed. Now she must acknowledge the error of the attempt. In the one dance that remained traditional she had seen the necessary break with the past. Not the one she had made, was always making; another thing entirely. A break with prescription and proscription. An alliance with the snake. She couldn't do it, she was too tired and riddled with fear. Her successor would have to begin again, as all successors had to do. The snake dance was winding to a close, reminding her of something she had heard or read in another world. Light years ago, scientists had snake-danced in a desert called Las Alamos, after the explosion of the first atom bomb. They celebrated the splitting of the atom with a spontaneous act of homage to the ambivalent snake, splitter of worlds, who had brought division into Eden.

She knew who would succeed her, who must succeed her. Their hands were upon her now, massaging for the last time. Now the Mystics would come, who worshipped the internal organs and above all the inner cavities of the body. She hardly cared if the Potter overheard her plans for the succession. After all, he could hardly object.

Yet perhaps he did object. Curie was yanked onto her bum and left to await the arrival of the Mystics without wine. Almost spitefully, a glass of cold water was pressed into her disappointed hand.

The Mystics seemed not to approach, simply to arrive. Their bodies were bare, like those of the Genitalics, but also unlike in that they were unbronzed and unpolished. They wore no fetishistic accessories. Nothing. Whatever glow they wore came from within. Their skin seemed almost transparent. Veins stood out, hearts were seen rather than heard to beat, muscles made themselves known without advertisement or flamboyance. There was a sense of retirement and reservation in the watchers. They were all taken inwards by the mystics.

It was hard to say what they did. They did nothing, yet they danced. They brought descriptions of the visions they had seen, and yet each M-other and Potter would have to give a different account of the vision which seemed to well up inside each individual beholder. They were philosophers who ventured not out of but into the cave. They were the mages who followed a star and found a child. The child lived, died and was reborn in each one of them, as the Mystics danced. The child was the same for all, yet different for each one.

Curie felt the child who was herself and not herself rise up and join in the dance, as others rose up and joined in alongside her. They whirled with dervish energy, both stately and abandoned. As she danced, Curie felt her loneliness leave her. All around her, the dead stirred and shook themselves and stretched. They glided amongst the living, shadowy but smiling, undemanding and unapologetic. They took up no space. They needed no time. They were simply there. Davy, Clare, Ruth, India, were with her and with these children, as they had been all along. She had not seen them before. She had not been ready before.

Now she was ready. She would go to the Mystics and afterwards to them, to her Companions. Not too long afterwards, she hoped. They faded from her as she yearned to join them, as if her yearning dispersed them. It was time for the ritual of the river, in which all the cults joined. There could be no vows of chastity in their world, though there were those, like herself, who reserved their sexuality for this annual ritual.

The Mystics sang as they turned towards the river. The song was a prelude to the GOB hymn, in which all voices joined. Curie felt certain of her path. She would inform them tonight of her decision, in the aftermath of their intimacy. No. That would load the aftermath with sadness. They would be tired. They would be sweetly sad with sleep and parting, after their dances and embraces. She would let them sleep tonight, and she would tell them tomorrow. She would make a good ending for their sake, for the sake of the children who had surpassed and outguessed her. Now she would retire in peace, and they would not continue to worship her after her retirement, after her death, as she had feared they might. They had seen through her. She would not block their future vision, not stand in their light.

The Mystic beside her lifted a sweet voice, sweet and high with the quivering purity of Gregorian plainchant. She sang too. It was the Hymn of the Body, the Hymn to the Oneness of the Gods of the Body. After it would come the ritual lovemaking in the river, and then she would retire to bed and, in her heart, to that stillness she so craved.

Still singing, they ran to the river. She let the children proceed her. She, too, would break with tradition, the tradition that she must lead them. Let them lead her. That was the better way round.

The song continued. It spoke of time, of how time was one and also multifarious. How long or short was a life, it asked. A long life could be feverish and feel like a day to the soul who had lived it. A short life might seem an eternity. Who lived long, who short? Impatience and restlessness could lengthen the shortest life. Energy, commitment, passion, could shorten the longest.

The leaders fell into the river. Others continued to fall in waves. Curie fell. The water was soft and warm. They would not begin the ritual until all were present. She peered into the darkness and saw, with a lightning-bolt of shock, that the Potters were with them. For the first time in their history, the Potters had entered the river with them. They meant to participate in the ritual lovemaking that must result in at least a handful of babies. It was usually much more productive than that, as if the Gods of the Body blessed the festivity with cherished consequence. But would they, could they cherish the consequences of this novel and dubious mating?

She was being pulled backwards, lightly but insistently. She resisted indignantly. Humility and its lessons were all very well. Long live the snake. Curie, like Lilith, would not make love in that position, especially when she didn't know the sex of her lover. It was protocol not to enquire, not to be fussy or particular, to take, as it were, what came. It was more than protocol, it was law, the law of the festival. But she did not have to lie back, to take it.

The pulling desisted. She struggled upwards to face her partner and found herself crumpling in laughter. It was the punch-line of the festival. Her partner was a Potter, of course, Sophia's Potter, the one who'd sat next to her on the grass, even touched her, gallantly making her acquaintance beforehand, though she hadn't realized it.

She couldn't stop now. It would scatter and confuse them. But was this small creature a woman or a man? A male or a female? Or both? Or neither?

Oral exploration was the safest. She indicated that the creature was to float on its back, and she approached her task, clammy with trepidation, but curious. As she did so, she felt something – some things, for there were hundreds of them, it seemed – silky and tongue-like, but thinner, tentacle-like, but not prehensile, simply wafting, stroking, the entrance to her vagina. The silk talons moved to her nipples, her ears, they were everywhere at once, and as she bent to her task, her mouth encountered labial folds, her fingers, greedy for answers, found space, walls, found a clitoris engorged, no, enlarged, big and hard as an early rosebud in her hands.

The creature continued its own exploration with the silky extensions of itself, and she continued hers. No wonder they overbred themselves, if their sex was like this! No wonder Sophia – but she censored the thought, having no wish to filter her pleasure through jealousy.

The great miracle of the festival was preparing in all their bodies. They prayed for it with their bodies, moving in one rhythm, begging the Gods of the Body for this token of their love, their cohesion, that they might all come together. It was never utterly, surreally unanimous. There were always a few howls and yells out of sync, like voices lagging after a great choir. As long as the choir was great, it didn't matter. It was a contribution, an echo.

They tensed. Messages ran madly around Curie's body. I shall appoint them both as my successors, she affirmed as the first shudders hit her. They were hitting her partner, too, she felt. Groans mounted around her, the water vibrated, and the air; the sky seemed to vibrate. The earth moved, they used to say. But the earth always moved. Even now. The difference was that you knew it, not as mere fact but as reality. You were part of it. *I am a part.* Curie breathed with the others.

They lay back under the stars. They bathed, they embraced with slow-motion heaviness, saturated with pleasure, with river, with one another. They swam out, slowly, and back to the shore where they would sleep. And in the morning, Curie promised Curie, in the morning, she promised the Gods of her tingling body, I shall announce my resignation, and my succession, and petition the Mystics to have me as a beginner. At least I know now that I am a beginner. At the same time, she reflected, it was her Nunc Dimittis, or the start of it. She lay on the shore and closed her eyes. The thought was not without comfort after the long, arduous night.

Dawn. They were a ragged band, a little settlement that had survived because of their devotion, their piety. Now they had outgrown devotion and piety, or would outgrow them soon, if the garment of their religion could not grow with them. It had never done so before. It had always remained essentially the same, demanding that the human being either shrink or go naked into life, religionless. That had been the only choice.

And now? Curie sat cross-legged, looking at her sleeping family. They slept like children after a Hallowe'en party, relieved of their pitiful costumes. The glory of the night was over. The glory of their defiance, their rebellion, was perhaps also finished. They would be gathered up again.

She went to wake Sophia and the Potter. They must be told first. They were sleeping together, lightly. They woke at a touch.

'It is time for me to go now,' she explained.

Sophia rubbed her eyes, and grabbed Curie's arm. 'Go where?' she asked in perplexity and panic. She shook her. 'Go where?'

'Soon, go – into the earth, and into the sky. Die,' she

said bluntly, tired of euphemisms. 'But first to the mystics. I have longed for years, to go to them.'

Sophia put her head into her hands and sat bowed. Around them heads were blossoming from sleep to bow like Sophia's, in prayer, Curie realized. She looked at the Potter. He shook his head at her, sadly.

'Did you not understand anything of last night,' Sophia demanded, lifting her head.

A murmur went up from the listening throng, a murmur that gave resonance to her anger.

'You cannot leave us now, for death, for mysticism, for anything,' she said impatiently. 'It is both too early and too late.'

'I did understand – something of it,' Curie replied. She was certain of her decision. 'I cannot stand as your Professor any more. It is for you –' she indicated the Potter – 'and you, Sophia. You must take my place.'

The crowd buzzed angrily. Curie was confused. They were angry with her, disappointed, rebellious. What could they want but her resignation, her withdrawal?

'You cannot,' Sophia repeated. 'I will not allow it and I will not succeed.'

'You refuse the succession?'

She nodded.

'And you?' Curie turned to the Potter.

'I refuse, M-other,' he replied, looking steadily into her eyes.

'But then what do you want of me?' she stammered.

'We wish you to really be our Professor,' Sophia said eagerly, 'to teach us that which you have withheld before. To tell us the story. The great story that you know and we do not.'

You do not know what you ask, she wanted to say. Wanted to say, but could not. It would only enrage them further. They could not know what they asked, because she had denied them the means. But the means were the telling, only the telling.

'I must recover – from the revelation of my own littleness.' Her eyes sought a mystic's. She needed an excuse to go away and die. Surely she could die, if she set her mind to it? She hid her face. The ultimate sin against the Gods of the Body. That which GOB was founded to prevent, to forbid by spirit and reason and light, whether suicide of the individual or of the mass.

She could hide it. They need never know.

Arms gripped her, ungently, took her hands down. It was the Potter. All the Potters were on their feet, buzzing and gesticulating angrily. She read the reason for their wrath in the face of her lover. They could hear what she thought.

He nodded. Now in his moment of ungentleness, she dubbed him officially male, with a wry smile for her own primitive sexism.

'Yes, we can read your mind,' he said. 'But we cannot piece together what we read. We make mistakes. We do not always find the truth we seek in the fragments we read. We need you to tell us, or it will be remembered wrong. They,' he gripped her wrists tight as she writhed away, 'your beloved companions, the ones whose graves you pray at but will not share though they are our M-others too' – he glanced at her face and his expression softened – 'they will be remembered wrong,' he went on firmly, but more gently. His hold relaxed. He had put the unarguable argument. 'You must see that that does not happen.'

'But the words,' she argued feebly. 'You will not understand the words.' Her own experience of the past night told her it was not so. The afternoon's adventures with Sophia, so long ago now, had told her it was not so.

'You will have Sophia with you as scribe,' the Potter continued. 'You are closest to her in all the Body.'

'When must I begin?' she asked tearfully.

'You are not a prisoner,' he said sorrowfully. 'It is not forced labour –'

'It is,' she replied. 'But perhaps not forced by you.' By the

63

terrible force against which she had fought for so long. By the truth.

'I must rest,' she wailed. 'I must wait, I must –'

There was silence. The sun was warm now. Could she rest with that prospect before her? Rest was for afterwards. If she waited, she would never begin.

Wearily, she rose to her feet. She summoned Sophia to her with a gesture. Slowly, shoulders slumped in resignation and defeat, she set out for her hut with the young woman beside her. Her heart thumped as they walked. Each step took her closer to that which she had never thought to face again. She could argue that that confrontation with shadows was suicide. But she would not. Delving into memory, reconstructing the past, might bring death. But it would not be death by suicide.

'Would it not be better,' she said spitefully, for she felt evilly spiteful towards this creature beside her, 'if I were to have as scribe one of the telepathic ones, one of the vocal ones?'

Sophia winced, then drew herself up. 'It would not be better. I shall take down everything you say, and – Germaine, the Potter – will relay it. He will know how best to do so. He has taught me,' she concluded sulkily. 'He can teach the rest. And you have taught me, too,' she added defiantly. 'And I can best assist you in your grief,' she said finally, flatly. 'Because I love you more than any other.'

Which way did she mean that? More than she loved the Potter, or more than any other loved Curie? The question was base, but she had to ask it.

Sophia smiled. 'More than I love any other,' she replied. 'Or will love any other.'

Curie took a step towards her. They had reached the wasteland, the scrub she so loved. With love, and hate – or anger, she amended – she must engender the story with an act of love. They lay on the ground, as the soft rain that always attended the end of the great festival began. It mingled with their wetness, a soft Autumn (One) rain. When they had each loved the other, they walked back to Curie's hut together. In silence they towelled each other. Sophia bent to make coffee for them, to prepare a breakfast, and Curie stopped her. Laughter bubbled up inside her.

'If you're going to be amanuensis to a writer of memoirs,' she said as Sophia frowned in her attempt to understand, 'you must not begin by doing the menial work, or you will end by doing nothing else.'

'I cannot cook?' Sophia tried to unravel the proposition. 'But I wish to nourish you, to help, to –'

'Sophia,' Curie said sternly. 'You are in great danger. These dangers recur and recur. I am learning. You must succeed me. One day, you must,' she overrode the protest that gathered in the young, tired face. 'You must be Professor equal to Germaine, and it is in your keeping that that precious equality lies. You see, it is not there for the asking.' She floundered for words. 'It is hard won. You may even now have a child in your body.'

Sophia nodded.

'You must fight to preserve your station, your dignity. Oh, let's begin.' Sophia looked more and more confused. She had never been without station and dignity. How could she appreciate the peril she stood in? It was another reason for undertaking the vast and excruciating project of describing the past. 'We will eat later, and I will cook,' Curie said resignedly. 'The water's boiled.' She mixed them the bitter root drink that passed for coffee in their world. She lit one of the herbal cheroots that were all they had to smoke.

Sophia took up her paper and her notebook. They no longer looked childish or old-fashioned.

Curie would have to go slowly. She must exclude nothing. She could not select for purposes of art, and yet she must give them a world. Where to begin?

She bowed her head and closed her eyes tightly. An image rose up behind them. She leant forward eagerly. The figures in the tableau were about to speak.

'I am the Lord thy God, thou shalt not have false gods before thee.' India looked up at the stained-glass window thoughtfully. 'We've started with the first commandment and broken them all.'

'Infidels,' Curie said carelessly, not caring to show that she was stung. Religion was her secret vice, mysticism her secret ambition. Or so she thought. 'Besides, who says what's false? And as for "Honour thy father and thy mother", scratch the missing father in my case, well I've done that. I've certainly honoured *her*,' she finished aggressively.

The four other women sprawled in the nave of the church turned to look at the window. Its pastel tones gleamed dully with a little mid-morning London light.

You might, at first glance, have credited Curie's assertion. Bee Fairchild, Curie's mother, martyr of Greenham Common, was certainly idealized in the glass. Whether it was an idealization meant to honour or to mock was an uneasy, second-glance question. Most disturbingly of all, it was far from clear what the creatrix herself had intended, or even whether she herself knew.

Bee was Venus rising from the sea. She stood naked, her blonde hair spilling and blowing around her. Her body was anonymously, regularly pleasing, like her features. She gazed off into space. There was no question of eye contact with her, or any contact. The grey-green light made her inhuman, amphibian. It was hard to say whether the slightly chartreuse luminosity of the background made her look supernatural or putrefying. The haloey light surrounding her certainly took more than a hint of phosphorescence from its tint.

India's eyes were also grey-green, with nothing sickly about them. They were troubled by the window. She had the most in common with Bee by background, and sometimes she had a guilty feeling that she knew her better than any of the others, particularly better than Curie. Her knowledge seemed almost criminal, almost carnal, like some kind of rape, imaginative and necrophiliac. Yet her guilt rested primarily in a sense that Bee was alive in her mind as she had never been in Curie's. She, India, had stolen something from Curie, something Bee's daughter strained to grasp, something which equally forcefully, almost magnetically, strained away and eluded her. India sometimes thought of her crime as mothernapping, as opposed to kidnapping.

The window proved beyond doubt that whether or not she comprehended Bee, Curie did not. India averted her eyes from it. She worked in geometric patterns and weaves. Like Bee, she suspected, she had a horror of the vulgarly literal, a horror that was moral as well as aesthetic. India's space in the church was hung with tapestries and rugs. Plants swung from woven slings like jumpers from parachutes. She lived quietly among her hangings like a doe in a forest, effectively camouflaged from the window and from Curie, whose private space was the choirloft beneath it.

Ruth hid herself, too, but brashly, behind large, fortress-like objects. Her workspace bordered India's sleeping quarters, and vice versa, an arrangement they found both private and companionable. India's workroom was as soft-textured as her bedroom, winking with broken mirrors, shiny bits and shells she insinuated into her creations. A bed in one, a loom in the other, distinguished them.

Ruth's studio was dominated by an enormous easel, behind which she spent most of her working hours, either standing to work or sitting to contemplate what she had done. Her bedroom held a tall full-length mirror and a huge four-poster bed. She had joined the posters with rope, and on this rope she hung her clothes. As she wore only smocks and baggy harem trousers, loose, vivid clothes, the scheme worked, though she had to sleep in the middle of the bed and her lovers complained of being tickled by the garments in the night, like strings made to dance on the head in the tunnel of love.

Ruth looked at the window with unequivocal hatred in her bold brown eyes. Curie had made its design a communal project when they first moved into the church. Bee belonged to them all. They would all have a say in her monument. Ruth, as it happened, had given a great deal of thought to the artistic presentation of twentieth century heroines and contemporary saints. Artistic, not autistic, she liked to say. Her eyes darkened as she regarded Bee, in whose image the proposition was certainly reversed.

Her own credo and aim was to create an impression of struggle and complexity in the expression on the face of the subject, rather than the usual embalmed banality. She had spent long, intense hours discussing her ideas with Curie. She ached to design the window, so much so that she forgot to tread warily.

Ruth addressed the taboo aspects of Bee's life and character. They were her frivolous, debby youth and the furtive, rebellious pregnancy she hid from her family almost until Curie was born. Bee claimed her family had deserted her, a claim they had always contested. She needed to think that, Ruth insisted, her eyes fixed on her vision of Bee instead of

69

on Curie. She needed to think so because she hungered and thirsted, not for justice but for martyrdom. She was an accident waiting to happen, a walking St Theresa complex. She went to Greenham because Greenham was obvious. The time and the woman coincided. None of this diminished or defined her. It made her real.

Curie listened and said nothing, but her eyes burned. She had written a biography that paid for the church they lived in and the food they ate. It was not the biography of the woman Ruth described. It had, perhaps, effectively buried that woman. It had sealed her human lips and given her the cold lips of an effigy, the cold stare of a statue. There had been some gentle criticism of it on that score, but not much. Bee was an object of guilt, of political superstition. It would not do to disturb her spirit. Let it sleep. The book was a bestseller. Curie's blue eyes blazed, then froze over as she heard Ruth out. She stood up, turned on her heel, and sought out Clare, to build the window.

Clare's eyes were clouded with resentful defeat when she looked at her handiwork. She was not there now, in the nave. They waited for her return. She had been broken by the window, or by Curie. Stained glass was one of her 'things'. She made cheerful little birds and other animals to be attached to ordinary windows, to give them some of the dark lustre of cathedrals, some of the sparkle of country churches. This was different. She worked according to whim, usually. Now she was overshadowed by Curie, playing the Most High to her conception. Curie had taken her over, instilling in her her own sense of the messianic Bee. She had failed to realize that Clare could be completely possessed, on both a rational and an intuitive level. The first took in and sought to give out again, in glass, everything Curie said about her mother. The second dealt more subversively with everything she did not say. Curie fell victim to the double edge of vacant possession, the peculiar eerie power of the possessed, eerie because it is neither conscious nor self-serving. It just is. Or Bee fell victim to it. The confusion of the eventual product was Curie's confusion, Curie's ambivalence, reproduced accurately and conscientiously. Clare had created a perfect reflection, not of Bee but of Curie's strange, haunted view of her.

Curie got both more and less than she had bargained for, Davy reflected, closing her eyes. Davy was a photographer. Her own suggestion had been that they work from photographs. Curie had listened and said no without a word, but Davy knew the wordless rejection was of her as well as of her craft. She shrugged, but the gesture was not as careless and assured as it once had been.

Davy was a second-generation atheist. She had lapsed from nonchalant atheism into a perilous state of Deus-envy since they had moved into the church. It was a double-pronged envy. She craved that which she had never known, and she craved the Unknown. For the first time in her adult life, the miraculous healing powers of the air brush, the transubstantiation of film into print, the hushed, expectant ethos of the darkroom itself, always sufficient to her sense of mystery before, were stale and poor.

For the first time, concurrently, she allowed a disused sense of romance and melodrama to overwhelm her pragmatic approach to human relationships. She had met Curie under totally genuine false circumstances. Curie had finally felt 'ready' to see the film of Bee's death at Greenham Common, one of the live tragedies of the age. There were always a few reporters present at the peace camp as things grew increasingly tense, with full alerts and half-alerts and practice alerts occurring almost weekly. On this particular day there had been a full alert, a mistake as it turned out later. An intelligence rumour was responsible. Bee, returning to the camp from a period of rest and reflection, didn't know the base was on alert and took a lighthearted (so they conjectured) opportunity to climb the fence. She had been in the act of planting one of five-year-old Curie's little

71

mittens on the fence, struggling to leave it raised in greeting, when she was first warned and then shot. The pale blue mitten, left totemically behind on the fence, was the last image on the screen. It was daubed with Bee's blood.

Curie saw the film through three times, then got up and left the studio without a word. Her silence was respected by the TV people but not by Davy who, having got wind of the story, literally burst from behind the stone lions that flanked the studio to get a good shot of Curie. She got it; a white face with unmistakably furious blue eyes.

The mask of fury that was Curie's face became demonic. She tore the camera from Davy's grasp and threw it into the street. She turned on Davy, kicked and bit and scratched until Davy managed to gain control. It took some minutes despite her fitness. Curie had the strength of a tiger. She collapsed on the pavement, sobbing and screaming her recriminations, not at Davy but at Bee. What made her angriest of all, from what Davy could make out, was the blue mitten with the red smear of blood on it.

'Why did she have to do that,' Curie spat. 'As if she did it for me. As if I had anything to do with it, or with her. She never spent longer than a weekend with me, if she could avoid it. What right did she have to take my mitten, to make it some kind of bloody symbol?'

Davy patted her head and took her home. She was hooked. Even the battered camera couldn't dissuade her from her vision of Curie in snarling, ferocious disarray. Davy, like Bee, was an accident waiting to happen.

She went on happening. She listened as Curie's original version of events underwent a whitewash. Bee emerged starched, immaculate and blank, as Curie became her inscrutable scribe. She was present when Curie found the church and began to plan the window. She was there when the others were invited to join the commune. She helped persuade them. She was there, but she was lost. It was her

72

own lostness that finally wrested her away from Curie, but not until she saw it reflected in Clare.

'Curie, Curie, wait,' Sophia said breathlessly. 'You must explain a little, just a few things.'

Curie held up a regal hand. 'I will explain in my own way,' she said imperiously, lit a cheroot and began. 'The five women in the church had one central thing in common,' she expostulated. 'A certain naiveté, not a simple variety, but a common one in our time. Clare was a magnified version of all of us,' she went on thoughtfully, 'as Davy, or any of us, might have realized, but didn't, of course. We all felt too superior to her. Only Davy was beginning to see the light, as she saw Clare succumb to me as she herself had succumbed – but she didn't realize she had taken on board my quasi-mystical leanings as well, also writ large in Clare –'

'Curie,' Sophia stood up and stamped her foot. 'This is gossip, when I asked you for fact, for definition.'

'Of course it's gossip,' Curie said absently. 'All history is gossip. Sit down, Sophia.'

Sophia sat down.

'As I was saying. Clare had been up and down the growth and guru circuits. She had tried every fringe religion going, grabbed every guru and held on for dear life. But dear life always prised her fingers loose again, and sent her spiralling into the abyss.

'So it was with all of us, in less lurid form. We had all reached some kind of impasse or spiritual ennui – no new worlds to be conquered by. We shared a sense of exhaustion and depletion which is itself, perhaps, the beginning of something else. But the something else depends on a willingness to stand and wait, rather than run away and deny that an end has been reached. It was at that point of nothingness, with the next conversion already shaping on the horizon, that Ruth might have painted her twentieth

73

century heroine, resisting its hypnotic draw. We felt we resisted and we were proud of it. Meanwhile we lived at Bee's glass feet in a church, working in a dilatory sort of way. It was pride that kept us from adding these elements together and realizing we had simply created a lunatic fringe of our own.'

Sophia cleared her throat.

Curie looked at her, over the tops of imaginary spectacles. 'Yes?'

'What is a guru?' She giggled. 'What a funny word.'

'I am a guru.'

'At that time,' Curie continued, 'there were many gurus. People wanted a way out of suffering, a way out of conflict. This is what the gurus offered them. They had various systems for eliminating the pain of living. Some were physical, even athletic. Some were contemplative. Some were both. There were ritual blood-lettings, physical and emotional, to bring about a ritual calm. Most of the gurus themselves were simply followers of fortune. In this they served their own followers well, for had they not been corrupt, they could not possibly have offered the simple answers those followers craved. In their material corruption, which they took no trouble to hide, they remained philosophically innocent. There was a kind of staggering obviousness about their statements which was taken for wisdom. The followers gave money, attention, time and loyalty, often hard work as well. They received security and that peace which not so much passes as evades understanding. It was a bargain.'

'And that was different from what had gone before?' Sophia frowned in concentration.

'Yes and no,' Curie replied. 'The corruption was no different in essence. The old religions were said to have traded on what would happen after you died. If you followed them, which included paying your tithes, you went to a place of bliss. If not – torment.'

74

'But surely no one believed that!'

'No,' Curie acknowledged. 'I don't think we did. I never met anyone who did. It was the escape from the mundane, the experience of the eternal in time, that people sought in religious experience. That and the continuity, the security, of a tradition.'

'Like our festivals,' Sophia said softly.

Curie nodded. 'That's right. A little bit of forever, breaking in on time and transforming it. A little bit of not-being-alone. Like sex. They always had a lot in common. There were some who didn't extract either sort of reward, the present or the future comfort, and they were the saints. They knew that virtue is, indeed, its own reward, and that that is the most desolate saying of all.

'The biggest difference between the old religions and the new ones was God. Many of the new ones did without him – yes, him,' Curie smiled. 'A him somewhere outside the body and the mind. Or many hims and hers, that was the older idea. Either way, God or the gods had always taken part in human life, actively interfered. Then they stopped. The old gods gossiped, manipulated, rewarded, punished, came down in all sorts of forms, including human, to be at the centre of human affairs. Then they, or he, seemed to lose interest. There were no more visits, no incarnations, no meddling, for all the pleas and prayers. Then came Auschwitz, and when even that failed to smoke him out, it was said that God was dead.'

'What was Auschwitz?'

Curie told her. The room was silent, as if the very walls and floors had to absorb the shock. Perhaps they could, as they could have absorbed blood or water into their mud. Sophia shook her head as though to reject what she heard, but she had forced Curie to speech, and she could not now refuse to hear what was said. She stopped writing and sat silent for some minutes, the pad on her lap. Their written language, a fanciful set of pictographs, was ill-suited to its burden. At length she picked up her pen, and spoke as she wrote her own words, not Curie's.

'The banality of good,' she said quietly. 'This is what we leave out. It is also just doing a job.'

'The banality of good,' Curie repeated in the same tone. 'That's what we rejected, you see, in our church. Evil could be banal – that reduced it very nicely. But good was supposed to be glamorous, or else it wasn't good. Let's return to the church now,' she said, more briskly.

'But there is one more big thing I don't understand,' Sophia objected. 'The Greenham Common, where Bee was killed, and why?'

'Not now, Sophia,' Curie answered tiredly. 'Enough horrors for now. Later.'

The five separate spaces in the church had evolved over time. The women had moved in with the idea that they would share and share alike. Not only that, but there would be no marking out or labelling of space. Everything would be everywhere.

Two months, a little less, and everyone was all over the place. Only the loo was separate, and Davy's darkroom. Surprisingly or not, Davy cracked first. She steamed out of her darkroom one Sunday, not the one I began with and will come back to, another Sunday, and delivered a sermon on order and self-indulgence. Most of their explosions happened on Sunday. Sundays without religion were restless, febrile days.

Davy pointed to their sluggish, sprawling bodies, their lack of boundaries of any sort. She commented on the perpetual twilight they maintained with alchohol and drugs.

'The Götterdämmerung,' she finished dramatically. 'There is no dawn around here. Dawn follows night, not elongated dusk.'

They yawned and stretched into position to respond. They were relieved to be relieved of their impossible ideals.

76

The impossibility had induced a creeping paralysis. They decided on a basic division of the church into kitchen, living space, sleeping space. It was very exciting. They had discovered rooms.

Curie was not excited. Curie was not relieved.

'It's the thin edge of the wedge,' she said gloomily. 'Next we'll be partitioning it into private spaces.'

They protested, far too much. Some three weeks later they were doing exactly that. The communal kitchen, which had been the sacristy, and the communal living room, which had been the sanctuary, remained as a sort of hub. Davy's darkroom, the old vestry on the other side of the sacristy, was somehow part of this central, forceful space. She was hidden, in her darkroom, from everyone; from Curie.

Curie's choirloft was the other pole of the church, exerting an opposite force. She refused to divide her work space from her bedroom, stubbornly holding to the old idea. She slept fitfully most of the time, with intermittent periods of dreamlike energy. She never worked. She had been unable to write since she finished her biography of Bee. She spent her long, somnambulist hours under Bee's fixed simper without looking up, as if the window were not there.

Clare followed Curie obediently in keeping her space integral. She had been unable to work since the completion of the window. But she kneaded bits of clay obsessively and made tiny little tikis and talismen perhaps intended to ward off Curie's evil eye. She lived in plain view of Curie and of the window, to the right of the sanctuary living room, and took no steps to protect herself other than shaping her pottery. It was as if no fortress or forest could shelter her.

'Broody, that's what you are,' was Ruth's comment on the little clay shapes. 'You should have a baby. Any sort will do. A sculpture. Even a meal.'

Clare smiled sadly. But Davy listened with attention,

77

and was soon to be seen shepherding Clare into the kitchen. Davy was the best cook of the five. Soon she spent as much time muttering to Clare amid the pots and pans as she did in the darkroom; and Clare, in the kitchen, was removed from Curie's gaze. She soon discovered that Davy's shoe-box-like little bedroom, formerly the generous closet where the silken vestments had hung, with the doors removed for ventilation, was even more hidden.

The other two made their arrangements, as described, and derived both pleasure and profit from them. Ruth and India worked. Davy, who had initially instigated the change, benefited least. She spent most of her time in the kitchen with Clare, the rest of her time in the shoebox of a bedroom, with Clare. She, too, was being taken over, though whether by pity for Clare or contempt for Curie was hard to say.

'The Trinity,' Ruth was heard to refer to them as (but only by India). 'Curie's the Father, Davy's the Son, and Clare's the Holy Ghost, only existing by the force of the passion between the other two.'

Curie waited, Davy waited, and Clare moved uneasily between the two of them. India and Ruth, to the extent that they were a captive audience, didn't wholly escape, either. They waited, like the others, for a resolution or a spontaneous combustion of some kind.

'Tongues of fire,' Ruth predicted. 'Crucifixion of the Son by the will of the Father. Tongues of fire, anyway.'

India smiled weakly and bent over her loom.

Then Clare began going out, and staying out. They had lived in the church as though on board a ship, venturing into the port only for provisions. That was part of the reason they failed to register Clare's excursions; it was unthinkable that anyone would actually go anywhere alone. They were all in it, whatever it was, together.

The other reason Clare's absence passed unnoticed was that her presence was so fragmented. Curie assumed she was with Davy, Davy assumed she was with Curie. The other two assumed she was with one or the other of them.

Curie had wandered into the kitchen this particular Sunday morning, possessed by a lapsed-Catholic fury. She had been raised not as a Catholic but as a lapsed Catholic, a religion in its own right. She wanted, as she stalked into the kitchen she hunted, a god to kill and eat. She was mixing herself a Bloody Mary when Davy came grumbling in.

'Not making one for Clare, I see,' Davy noted. 'Does she have to subsist on love?'

'I wouldn't know what she subsists on,' Curie returned. 'The formaldehyde you pickle your victims in in that darkroom of yours, I presume.'

'At least my victims are only pictures,' Davy sparred.

'Have you flattened her then, in bed,' Curie asked sweetly, 'into a picture? Poor Clare.'

'We don't do that,' Davy informed her. 'Didn't do that, that is, when we did do – other things. Unfortunately, Clare's taste isn't as good as her flavour. That's why she prefers you. What a waste, when all you want is a trampoline. –'

'What do you mean, prefers me?' Curie demanded, and took a bloody swig of Mary. 'She's with you right now.'

'Don't be dafter than you are, you old cow, she's with you now.'

'She is not.'

India came into the kitchen and wished she hadn't. She was just about to leave when Davy stopped her.

'India, have you seen Clare?'

She stopped. 'Have *I* seen Clare,' she echoed, confused. 'No, of course I haven't.'

'Neither have I,' Davy said flatly. 'All night or this morning.'

'Neither have I,' Curie said sharply, and started mixing herself another Bloody Mary.

79

'I'll have one of those, Curie,' Ruth stuck her head in to request. 'I've been out here eavesdropping, as usual. I haven't seen the Holy Ghost either, lately.'

She sputtered when she sipped her Bloody Mary, which was fierier than usual with Tabasco. By then they were seated in the sanctuary, at the beginning of the chapter.

'Curie,' Sophia sputtered as though she, too, had been over-exposed to Tabasco, 'how can they be seated at the beginning of the chapter?'

'Easily. That's where they are seated when Clare walks in and –'

'Curie, wait. You said at the beginning of the chapter that they were seated in the nave, not the sanctuary. So how can they be seated in the sanctuary now and still be at the beginning of the chapter?'

'Change it for me, will you?'

'But Curie, why did you not seat them in the sanctuary at the beginning of the chapter?'

'Because I hadn't come to the part about the living room being the sanctuary yet.'

'But you knew it was. You remembered. Or did you forget, was that it?'

'Forget? Oh, I hadn't decided yet.'

'But Curie, you are not deciding, only remembering.'

'No, Sophia, I am deciding. I am deciding how to tell you what I remember, what images and symbols to use. The characters, yes, I am remembering. The rest –'

'You are inventing?'

'Not entirely, Sophia, not entirely,' Curie patted her hand comfortingly. 'Now let's get back to the sanctuary, shall we?'

As Ruth was sputtering over her Bloody Mary, Clare walked in. She looked around at them and smiled to herself.

'Same old Sunday, I see,' she said disparagingly.

'Where the hell have you been?' Davy growled. 'We've been frantic.'

'I must say you look it. It never occurred to you I might have somewhere to go, something to do? Simple as that.'

'But what?' Curie asked wonderingly.

'Well might you ask. I wasn't screwing and I wasn't sleeping and I wasn't finding God. Or losing God. What else is there?'

'Politics,' Davy said heavily. 'You've found politics.'

Clare hesitated for a moment, seemed to be thinking. Her blonde hair caught the light and gleamed, blondely, questionably.

'Questionably,' Sophia interjected. 'Why "questionably"?'

'It is questionable to mention blonde hair gleaming blondely,' Curie replied.

'It does sound pretty terrible,' Sophia agreed readily. 'Shall we change it to –'

'I don't mean the style is questionable,' Curie said patiently. 'I mean it is extremely dubious to mention blonde hair at all.'

'Blonde hair?' Sophia's fingers went, irresistibly, to her own shining blonde bob. 'Why is it questionable? Is brown hair questionable?'

'No.'

'Is grey hair questionable, M-other?' Sophia asked, provocatively formal. 'Grey hair, like yours, is that questionable?'

Curie shook her head.

'I see,' Sophia nodded. Her voice held controlled fury. 'Only blonde hair is questionable.'

'That's right,' Curie nodded in turn, and beamed almost playfully.

'But why?' Sophia screeched, a rather hoarse screech. 'Why?'

81

'Because,' Curie explained calmly, 'At the time, blonde hair was a symbol of everything –'

'A symbol of everything,' Sophia drawled in pleased astonishment. Her hand went to her head again.

'Everything tawdry and empty and glamorous,' Curie continued curtly. 'Brown hair was the banality of good. Blonde hair meant – went with – big tits and no brain.'

'But everyone has a bi –'

'I don't mean literally. There was an expression, "A dumb blonde" – you see?'

Sophia was quiet for a second, and when she spoke it was with great decisiveness. 'Make her a brownette.'

'Brunette. I can't, Sophia.'

'Why not?'

'Because she wasn't a brunette.'

'But you are deciding, not remembering, what images and symbols to use,' Sophia recited. 'Why use a blonde one if it is so dangerous?'

'I told you, I was remembering the characters. Clare's character –' Curie hesitated. 'She was a blonde character,' she said finally. 'Not a brunette one. A brunette Clare would have had another life. Everything would have been different. She was blonde.'

'So, Curie, now biology is destiny,' Sophia said, startlingly. 'You are being very questionable indeed.'

'Look, I already have her standing there with the light shining on her blonde hair blondely or whatever –'

'I can change it,' Sophia said blandly. 'I can make the light blonde, not the hair.'

'Sophia, don't you dare –'

'Light is blonde, is it not?' Sophia went on pleasantly. 'It is not brunette, it is blonde. A sign of favour, then, to have hair like light. I think she'll stay a blonde.' She waited.

Curie took a deep breath and continued.

✳

'Clare,' India said gently. 'Would you like something to eat or drink?'

Clare shook her head. 'Thanks, India, I'm fasting.'

'Fasting,' Davy queried, 'I thought you'd found politics?'

'I don't think I actually said. But are you implying there are no political grounds for undertaking a fast?'

Davy sighed.

'This place,' Clare continued, turning around and taking it in from every angle, 'is so strange to come back to. From the real world, I mean,' she went on. 'You know, the one out there.'

'We know,' Davy muttered. 'But who says it's real?'

'Isn't that what your photographs show? Don't tell me you've lost faith in reality too, Davy.'

There was real concern in her tone. Curie wheeled and faced her.

'What do you mean, "too"?'

'Oh, well, Curie,' she sighed sympathetically. 'I don't suppose you and reality have ever been introduced.'

'I suppose you're going to introduce us?'

Clare drew a long breath. 'I'm going to try, Curie. I'm going to try.'

Then she struck. They were unprepared for the accuracy of the strike. They believed she was converted to politics. They believed politics was less lethal than religion. The real snake poison was religion, or sex; not politics.

So they listened without apprehension, and they were acted upon by her words. Their own unguarded lassitude was part of it, and the guilt that lassitude induced. The Bloody Marys were part of it. Sunday was part of it. Bee Fairchild was part of it. And Clare was very much part of it.

'We've come to a dead halt here, under the window,' she began.

'Comrades,' Curie said weakly, but without conviction. It was too true to be penetrable by a heckle. Clare knew a rule of sermonizing; always start with a self-evident truth.

'We're mesmerised,' she went on, 'hypnotized. Under a spell, under glass, that's how we live – under glass.'

'Under glass,' India repeated dreamily, then looked around, embarrassed.

'We're ruled by an ideal we can never achieve, frozen by our failure like flies in amber. Frozen before the spectre of failure,' she raised her eyes to the window, 'A spectre we'll do anything not to see – including drink,' she pronounced the word with a disgust that made India, a moderate drinker, wince.

'Or blow dope – well-named, dope,' she went on. 'Anything, anything, to escape her scrutiny. But we do not escape, because she is in each one of us, in the shape of an idea, an idea of perfection from which we flee in terror.

'Well, we should be terrified,' she smiled at them suddenly. The effect was electrifying. 'Perfection is terrifying. Failure is terrifying. And we must risk both. Or die in our souls.

'I have a scheme,' she thundered at them. 'To misquote another perfectionist. I have a scheme, not a dream. A scheme such as Bee Fairchild might have engendered. Perhaps she inspired me. Of course she inspired me!

'Do you remember the story of Scheherazade?' she asked conversationally. 'A certain macho sultan also had a scheme. His scheme was to save himself from betrayal and humiliation. In order to assure that his wife was faithful to him, utterly and entirely faithful, he resolved to marry every evening and have his bride slain every morning. Faithfully.

'Does it sound familiar? Can you think of anyone, of many ones, who are determined to slay their bride, their – and our – consort and mother earth in order to dominate her completely? Because they cannot bear for her to retain a single secret, a single mystery, they will blow her, and us, to kingdom come.

'Back to the sultan. The daughter of his valet, Scheherazade, begged her father to allow her to marry the wretched man. Her methods of persuasion were masterful.'

'Mistressful,' corrected Curie.

'Get stuffed, Curie,' corrected Ruth.

'She had a plan, a scheme, too,' Clare let her voice drop dramatically. 'She would tell tales in the night, such tales that the sultan would not be able to kill her at dawn like the others because he would have to know the end of the story, which only she could tell. It worked – for one hundred-and-one nights, as you know. And by then the sultan was brought to see the error of his ways.'

'Well?' Davy spoke up gruffly, trying to break the spell.

'Well – why not try it?'

'Try what?' Ruth asked eagerly. She was bitten. 'What?'

'Scheherazade's scheme. On our sultan, in his nuclear bunker, about to blow us all to blazes.'

'Tell stories,' Curie breathed. 'To the men in the bunkers –'

'With their fingers on the buttons,' Clare nodded, not wanting to be pre-empted. 'It's no use talking to the leaders, they can't hear anything. But the ordinary men who have to fire the missiles are different.'

'But the sultan executed his bride every morning,' Davy objected. 'We don't know when –'

'Oh, yes we do,' Clare said excitedly, 'Oh, yes, we do!'

She took a deep breath. 'My political cell has very good intelligence. They know the day and the hour.'

'But what if it isn't,' India stage-whispered into the silence.

It was Clare's cue. She turned to face her. 'But India,' she whispered back, 'what if it is?'

They went on talking through the night, arguing. But Operation Scheherazade was underway. Everything else had been tried, Clare said steadily, looking at the window. And if nothing happened that day three months and a bit hence, well, what did it matter? They would have done something. They would have started.

They argued practicalities. They wouldn't be allowed anywhere near the bases.

85

'We're going to turn into drabs overnight like reverse Cinderellas,' Clare replied. 'Into conventional women. Then we're splitting up. There are five nuclear bases in this country.'

'More fairy tales,' growled Davy. 'You'll be saying it's numerology next. Five bases.'

Clare's eyes flickered. 'Maybe it is.'

They debated, but they were only playing with the idea, relishing it.

'My name,' Curie said sadly.

'But we'll all change our names, silly.' It was Ruth who replied.

It was too late to object. It had been too late, ever since the blonde bombshell had dropped it in their midst.

'Curie,' Sophia said impatiently. Hurry up and tell me, I want this story to go on. What is "bombshell"?'

'I guess this is the point at which you have to know,' Curie said heavily, 'for the the rest to make sense. But after I tell you, I want to go on to the end without interruptions, all right?'

Sophia nodded.

Curie told.

'But Curie, what is a blonde bombshell?'

'An expression. It means the impact of the beautiful blonde is like —'

Sophia's face expressed repugnance at the idea. 'But this is a great insult, Curie.'

'No, Sophia, it was not considered an insult. It was considered the opposite.'

'I do not understand,' Sophia pushed the notebooks off her lap in irritation. 'I do not understand these dumb blondes who think it is clever to be like these bombshells that blow people into — into —' her lip trembled. 'I do not understand the world that made these things.'

'Neither do I.'

'But you must. You must. Why did they? What for, what did they think, how did they think?'

'Sophia,' Curie held out her arms. 'You are very tired, and so am I.'

'We have been sleeping every night,' Sophia said crossly.

Curie nodded. 'Indeed we have and that is why you are so frustrated. That and because you do not understand. One I can do nothing about. The other, I can. So come and be my dumb blonde, come, blonde bombshell, and explode with me.'

'Curie, you should not talk to me like that.'

'No,' Curie agreed. 'I should not.'

'It is power. That is it, isn't it? Everything? The sultan and the blonde question and the bombshell?'

'Yes.'

'And even now?'

'And even now.'

'But who will win,' Sophia wailed. 'I am lost.'

'You will win.'

'Oh, no, Curie. *You* will win.'

Curie looked at her and laughed. Sophia laughed back at her. The war began, to see who would lose first, who win last.

'Now, Sophia, through to the end,' Curie reminded her. They lay side by side sipping coffee.

Sophia nodded languorously, picked up her notebook and pen with a long, sweeping arm, from the floor beside the bed. The finished books were collected every dusk. Dusk was gathering earlier these days.

'Autumn (Two) already,' she yawned. 'Soon the dusks will come late again, soon more light,' she said enthusiastically.

Curie nodded sadly. 'The first task,' she began, 'was to turn ourselves into respectable women in the shortest possible time, change our names and each head for a nuclear base, there to persuade the commandant to allow us to read a little to the men to whom she and everyone owed so much. Such a quaint English notion. Of course we would write our own tales, really. The exercise had to belong entirely to us, and the responsibility for its outcome. But we'd carry volumes of Dickens and the Brontës, famous stories,' Curie interpolated hastily. 'And we'd memorize our own.'

'They're armed,' Davy enjoyed reminding them at intervals. 'We could be shot.'

'Like Bee Fairchild,' someone, not Curie, commented.

'We'll never stop them with fairy tales,' Davy the Devil's advocate insisted.

'It stopped the sultan,' Ruth pointed out.

'But that's a fairy tale,' Davy remained inexorably logical.

'What if the date isn't even the date?' Curie added her voice. 'It's all a bit of crying wolf, isn't it?'

'Did Bee Fairchild cry wolf?' Clare asked rhetorically. 'Do all the Greenham women cry wolf?'

With many such exchanges, they set about the task of making themselves over. The church became a dormitory. Acoustics meant for sublimity proved ideal for ridicule and self-ridicule. None of them had ever indulged in makeup, curling irons, ladies' razors, silk stockings or perfume, except for the odd hint of musk or patchouli. Now they bought Femme, and shared it out. They doodled on their faces, they dawdled in the bath. They discovered that femininity was staggeringly time-consuming.

'I never have time to paint any more,' Ruth complained. 'I *am* my self-portrait.'

'It makes us look older,' Davy observed.

'It makes us look deader,' Ruth capped.

'It was invented as an embalming technique, after all,' Clare said instructively, 'to give an appearance of life to the dead.'

'Make-up,' India said softly. 'An imitation of life. It insinuates deadness. It always reminds me of the window,' she finished lazily. They found themselves sneaking looks at the window. There was no denying that they resembled Bee Fairchild far more now than they ever had before.

But who was she imitating? Who was the first one, the first real woman? Eve? Did a full range of cosmetics come with the loincloths, after the Fall? Most probably.

The world met them differently. They were acknowledged and approved when once the best they could have hoped for was a resigned: Oh, one of *them*.

'It's a fiction of a sort,' Curie said dreamily. 'Like your self-portrait,' she nodded to Ruth. 'You're fascinated and distracted and finally obsessed with the image in the mirror like a character in a novel. There is nothing else.'

They were transformed. They had their masks and characters down pat. Ruth, who preferred exaggeration and extremes, was a big blowzy matron who wore a chinstrap and eyeshade to bed.

'Kinky,' Davy commented, and was pinched for her pains.

Ruth called herself Alice Lord.

'Bit o' class,' she preened. 'I'm a snob, you see. Oh, I do so loathe myself. Spinsterish snotty distressed gentlewoman who loves to meddle.'

'That'll be easy to play,' Davy commented, and was more convincingly pinched. She and Ruth had become very friendly during the auditions, as they called their nightly performances of themselves as they would be.

'Auditioning for life,' Clare said dramatically. 'In more ways than one.'

She was taking the role of a pale, devout creature called Felicity Hay. They all thought it sounded peculiar, but then, so many names did.

India remained herself. She called that self Rebecca Forrester, but she was still India. She had always been camouflaged among her plants and hangings. She was no more so now, as a teacher of weaving. She had found a job near 'her' base, teaching evening classes.

Davy was someone else entirely. She had turned herself into a demure gamin, a model instead of a photographer, and was in every other way her own alter ego. She monopolized the bathroom, soaked herself, painted her fingernails. She baptized herself Christine (Chris) Moriarity, and affected a soft brogue.

Curie had taken a place as a student near 'her' base, and cultivated the image of an earnest bluestocking. Susan

Winter slipped easily into her role, so easily as to almost, for a time, sink beneath it.

'Curie,' Sophia said intently, 'Curie, I know I said I wouldn't interrupt, but Curie, I need to know this thing.'

'Thing?' Curie looked around with an absent-minded smile. 'Winter,' she murmured. 'I wonder why I ever –'

'Curie, what happened to the window?'

'Window?'

'The window, Curie, in the church. The blonde anti-bombshell. But dumb. Mute. In every sense. Curie, what happened to the window?'

Curie sighed. 'Just when I was remembering Winter,' she began petulantly, then caught sight of Sophia's face. 'Sophia, what makes you think there was a window?' She asked gently, almost tenderly.

'What?'

'I needed something to make you see – and I thought, what you see through is a window. Ergo – a window. I created it. For you to see through. For you to understand Bee Fairchild and all the complicated and exaggerated feelings around her.'

'There was no window?' Sophia whispered.

'There was no window,' Curie smiled.

Sophia leaned forward and punched her in the nose.

'Sophia,' Curie shrieked, 'in the name of both our bodies' gods –'

'That is what you did to me, but worse. I am defending my honour, which you have impunned,' she pronounced haughtily.

'Impugned,' Curie went to wash her face. 'Well. Sophia –' she turned, a washcloth held to her nose. 'It's poetic licence. Shorthand. I had to find a shortcut for you through years and years of background. The shortcut was a window.'

'But there was no window,' Sophia said gloomily. 'So there was no shortcut.'

91

'But there was, it did, you understood, you saw through it –'

'If I saw through it, it existed.'

'Of course it existed, while you were seeing through it. It still exists, for you.'

'Curie –' Sophia brought her fist down, trembling, and smashed it against the bed. 'You are confusing me. It exists. It doesn't exist. Then it exists again. What can I tell them all, the M-others and the Potters, for whom the window exists?'

'Sophia,' Curie said softly, 'There was a window.'

Sophia closed her eyes.

'But not that window. There was a window on a side aisle, the same side as Davy's darkroom and bedroom – her dark rooms,' she laughed, a young laugh. 'A stained-glass representation of a female saint. I never knew which one. A blonde saint. In my mind it became confused with Bee. I was a little bit in love and a little bit in hate with the idea of her. I hardly remembered her, it was mostly the idea. And I fastened my love and my hate onto that insipid window. And when I came to tell you the story, I fastened on it again, changed it, enlarged it.

'I had staring contests with her,' Curie went on. 'She always won. Unblinking glass eyes. I turned the window of my obsession into your window, do you see?'

'And is it gone, your obsession?'

'I believe it is.'

'At my expense,' Sophia said icily.

'Sophia – can I tell you something else? In the story of Scheherazade there's another bit. You see, it isn't actually the sultan Scheherazade tells her stories to, not directly. She gets his permission to bring her sister with her, to say goodbye. She tells the stories to her sister, who sleeps at the bottom of the bed, and the sultan overhears. Now, I always thought that was very clever, if a little unconventional for a wedding night. Because the sultan would be much more curious when he was overhearing a story told to someone else. We did it in the bunkers by telling the first half of the story directly to one man, the second half to the other.' Curie paused. 'The other thing is, with her sister there, Scheherazade never had to be at a loss, and lose her head. If she got stuck, her sister could finish the story. Do you understand what I am saying, Sophia?'

'But, Curie,' Sophia whispered, frightened, 'I do not know the story.'

'But you know what happened to the window, Sophia. As well as I do. What did they do with the window, Sophia, when they sold the church?'

Sophia covered her face with her hands for a long moment.

'It's all right if some of your own tension gets into your story,' Curie told her. 'You need tension.'

'Curie, please do not interrupt when I am building atmosphere,' Sophia protested. She was silent again. 'They left it,' she said finally. 'And they forgot it.'

'They left it. And they forgot it. Forgot it. Forgot it! Who do you think you are, Sophia, Ernest Hemingway? For this you build atmosphere? "They left it. And then they forgot it"?' Curie stood with her backside against the sink, holding her pink nose as if in disgust.

'Isn't it good?'

'It's terrible. I built up a whole ethos, a whole mythology about this window–'

'Which doesn't exist –'

'Neither did the gods of mythology, the gods of the Old and New Testaments, the –'

'How do you know?'

'What?'

'You think they didn't exist because they fell silent. Maybe – maybe they were tired, or depressed – too depressed, too shocked to speak. They're still in shock, the gods.'

'Then they wouldn't be gods.'

93

'Maybe the only thing they could say would be the end of us and they are using all their god-energy and their god-power to keep from speaking that last word. They hear us begging, screaming for extinction, for you tell me of a people screaming for extinction – and they are mute, because they still believe in us. They wait.'

Curie looked out the window at the wasteland. 'You know, I can see my window,' she commented. 'It is so very real to me – that I can see it.' She smiled.

'But you are perverse, Curie. Just because you can see it doesn't prove it doesn't exist.'

'No. Not just because I can see it,' Curie conceded.

'I do not think you can see these gods, anyway. Can you?'

'No.'

'There, you see?'

'No.'

'Never mind, M-other. Put your head in my lap and I will tell you something.'

'Sophia, you're becoming a bully. First you punch me and now you push me. What is it that you want to tell me?'

'A secret. You do not understand everything, Curie.'

'That isn't a secret, Sophia.'

'It was a secret from me. And I think a secret from you. Don't skulk, Curie.'

'Sulk, Sophia. Skulk is – hide in shadow.'

'Don't skulk, Curie. The window is gone now, there is nowhere to hide – did the window in the aisle not look a little bit like Davy, too?' Sophia laughed.

'A little, maybe.'

'And I shall be the last of your blondes. Now, Curie, I will pretend your head is a book on my lap, only a book. Now there must be only the story.'

'But Sophia – how will you write?'

'All right. Side by side then, we sit. Like children. And there is still only the story. Curie, your head cannot be a book on my shoulder, it is too unlikely.'

'I was just thinking how young you are.'

'Curie, please. I may be young, but you are turning juvenile.'

'It's a privilege of age. And these herbs –' Curie sniffed the cushion under her head. 'How glad I am that they survived into this world.'

'Curie, you are talking rubbish. You do not wish to go on, do you?'

'No,' Curie said in a small voice.

'"I was just thinking how young you are",' Sophia mocked. '"Oh, these herbs –"' she sniffed her pillow.

'Sophia, you look like a pig after truffles, and if you never saw such a thing, neither did I. It's an insult. All right.' Curie sat upright, crossed her legs. 'Yes. It does get tricky. Never mind, "nothing became her life like the telling of it".'

'You have recovered your vanity and your sanity at once,' Sophia settled beside her. '"How young you are"! "Oh herbs"!' She snuffled again and was rewarded with a dig in the ribs.

'It was Ruth who initiated Scheherazade. She approached the base with beaming good humour and basketfuls of fruit from her allotment like little Red Riding Hood – never mind. The men were extremely touched. They were tired of their unpopularity. Not that the locals didn't like them, they did; after all, they brought jobs and something more fundamental, self-importance, to the locale. That's what jobs gave, really. Rich people didn't feel the lack of them, or at least they didn't feel their confidence ebbing away if they didn't work, because they knew they had importance. Their money and position gave it to them. Other people got their money and their position from their jobs, and so those jobs were important.

'But the base had been placed in their village, rather than another. They had been selected. Remember, even

95

disease can make someone feel important, and the attention that goes with it from experts. There were plenty of experts, suddenly, and they all wore uniforms, which made it all the more important.

'But nationally they were neither welcomed nor liked, and they knew it. It upset them. They knew that many people in this small, funny country which duty forced them to live in thought they were callous and brutal and ignorant. They were sensitive about that.

'So the fact that Ruth, Alice, rather, was not a native of the vicinity was rather in her favour with the base, if not with the actual locals. But she kept out of their way. They might just see through her, as the Americans would not. She was maternal with the Americans. Not sexy. And she wrote a "Come on in, the water's fine" letter to the others, a sort of epistle, advising them to be the same. Not sexy, she insisted.

'A charming English notion, the men thought, and it warmed them in the damp, chilly country where they found themselves. Each base commander agreed the scheme without reporting it or confiding in his colleagues. Just a quirky sort of compliment to him alone.

'The day came that Clare's group had said would be the last. By now the women were deeply into unreality. Even if they had not been, how real could life be on the last day?'

'Like every day,' Sophia said piously.

Curie lifted her hand to her mouth and bit it. Sophia let out a little screech and sucked it noisily.

They had discovered another facet of unreality. Only three of the bases were real, and no one except the commanders knew which ones they were. Two were dummies. Two buttons pushed nothing, connected nothing. But even in these fake bunkers, the guns were real. They could die in these, as in the others.

It was also clever. 'The lady or the tiger,' the commanders said, laughing. The women felt Scheherazade was at home amid such Byzantine logic. The men, it was explained, were spared a moral decision. It was Russian roulette. It was, though no commander would have been so crude, like having an abortion without knowing whether you were pregnant.

The men would be spared any side effects, any sleepless nights, breakdowns, remorse. No one had responsibility, explained the commandants, other than 'Supreme Command' – and it was difficult to know whom or what they meant.

The men ceased to exist as moral beings. The women understood that much. They were extinguished, in the bunkers. That perhaps made them different from the sultan, perhaps not. Was he in any sense a moral being, as a perpetrator of daily murders? Probably not. Yet, after the thousand and one nights, he became one – and they had only this one day.

It isn't my grave, it's theirs, Ruth thought as she followed the commander down into the ground. Those men have no knowledge and no choice. They've gone back into chaos already, down here.

They all had similar thoughts. Thoughts passed between them, through the metal and the miles. The metal corridors were alike, mocking halls of mirrors, steel reflections blurred and twisted. They knew, now, something of the blandishments of security and acceptance. They understood more of what they were up against. They knew something of how lost these men were, something of the intricate, labyrinthine games that had been played with their minds. They were far less inclined to judge them than they once had been.

They felt the icy quality of the machine into which they had inserted themselves. They felt its utter rigidity, how any compromise represented collapse and impotence. They felt their own outrageousness within it. They felt guilt; they were impostors. They felt despair. Their little scheme was piddling, absurd. Fiddling while Rome burned. They were villains as they walked as if to the stake or the gallows, confession on the tip of each tongue.

The white, deaf missiles were rampant above them, triumphant. Nothing could deter or stop them. What were they doing here, when they could be – ? What could they be doing? They swallowed, remembering their stories, remembering each other's stories. They had each memorized them all, with all the rehearsals in the church.

They remembered the church, as they walked those cold underground miles. Their lives there. Their lives. Scheherazade had had it easy. Her responsibility was small. Then again, did she feel responsible, or guilty? Certainly not. She was taking a chance. It made a hell of a good story.

They were smiling shyly when they arrived, wishing they could be swathed and veiled like their namesake. The uniformed men around them had an advantage. Maybe if all else fails, the women thought, we could seduce them. But no. Sex was no rival here. So much Scheherazade had known. Death was the bigger kick for these sultans. She had her sister! they wailed in their hearts. So do we, they answered themselves. They took deep breaths at the entrances to the tragic little playrooms, at the sight of the boy-men inside. The five-strong secret Order of Scheherazade were installed, three in nuclear bunkers, two in duds. It wouldn't matter, and besides, maybe the men had the same choices. Maybe moral choice couldn't be taken from them. No one had yet thought to make toys of these bunkers, with plastic men inside, for children to play with. Or of the shelters in the gardens either, with miniature stockpiles of food and ammunition. Not yet.

In three nuclear bunkers and two bluffs, a woman shook hands with two men, noting the temperature of their eyes, the humidity of their palms. Then she sat down, and began.

98

✑ Ruth's Tale

Remember the publicity campaign for the *S.S.Watercress*? She was a pleasure liner. Built for leisure, the glossy illustrations read. Sails like a snail, they promised, underneath magnificent enlargements of a snail in full sail, with a locus of whitewash behind . . . no? I was hypnotized. Even now it's hard for me to say exactly why.

Snails were the friends of my childhood. They didn't run away like tortoises, or die like robins. I put the tortoises by the garden shed, with screens round to make them a lovely, rather Japanese sort of environment. They always bolted, if tortoises could be said to bolt. At any rate, come morning they were gone. The screens were pushed down and trodden on, you could tell by the depressions in the mesh, by a gentle but determined tortoise.

My favourites, my familiars, were the slow dull creatures, not the quick flashy ones. I loved watching birds, but only the wounded ones were my compatriots. Despite this kinship under the skin, or broken bone, I was left alone by them, too, in the course of their first nights under my roof. The roofs I constructed for robins were also screen, were in fact the same ill-fated screens. The screen roof was in place, come the dawn. The robin lay cold and stiffened beneath it.

I was perplexed, not to say tormented. There were also elephants and whales – oh, I loved whales with a hopeless, a tragic passion. I longed for a glimpse, for a note of the legendary song from the shy but imposing diva of the high seas. I had an almost Ahab-like thing about them, but in my case it was not a destructive obsession. The whale had taken my heart, not my leg, and I wished only to witness, to worship at its magic rustling fountains. Something of me was with them. If they were lost from the world as a breed, a bit of me would disappear with them. It was vested in no other reality but theirs. A piece of reality itself would crumble, if the whales should vanish. The world would become less real.

Somehow I understood this from a very early age. I made it my life's work to attempt to save them. It seemed to many a blinkered career, a minor concern to preoccupy my one lifetime. Their criticism seemed to me equally blinkered. No one of us could hope to save everyone, or every species. I felt what the loss of the whale would mean. I *knew*. Hence I was fitted to work for their rescue and continuity. I had recognized, without being able to name it (for I am no Aristotelian prodigy) the likeness between us, unlike as we were. I called my recognition love, and I still do.

Dolphins, of course, I respected and admired, the Good Samaritans of the deep, always as ready for a race with an ocean liner as they were to force a suicidal swimmer back to shore. They never lost their races out of pity or politeness, either, nor left the swimmer to her own devices, should she resist their forceful nudges. They knew better for the best of all reasons, because they were tempted towards suicide themselves, *in extremis*.

I wasn't a vegetarian, but there were things I wouldn't eat. Chicken, turkey, I cut into with relish, slung the drumsticks happily over my shoulder. My indifference was aesthetic. They were ugly creatures. I could feel no compunction on their behalf. Cows didn't excite my compassion either, though calves did. I drew the line at veal like many a good hypocrite. Rainbow trout, salmon, mackerel, I couldn't touch. They were too beautiful. They were plucked like birds from the sky with the cruel use of hooks and poor skewered worms. Ugh, no. Crustacea were far too curiously made to deserve being served up as mere sustenance. Shellfish in general, like all the fruits of the sea, were simply too beautiful to eat, though I cheerfully consumed the daintiest apricot from the tree. I am not pretending to describe a consistent or in any way exemplary moral stance on these things. I am simply doing some moral scene-setting, presenting my own particular quirks without further comment.

I've come a long way from snails! Maybe that's where my protective feeling developed from. At any rate, they were gregarious creatures, generous with their time. My parents, luckily, agreed with me that gardens benefited most from a regime of benign neglect, along with children. The snails and I flourished together.

It fascinated me that they were both terrestrial and marine. I walked upon land all day, but at night I often found myself at sea. Anything might happen. I might meet any sort of strange, beautiful creature. When I wept, it was sea water that splashed my face. I could taste it. I, too, was a creature of land and sea. In fact, as I learned in school, I was mostly made of water.

That is, in fact, the only thing I remember learning in school. Perhaps it was enough. Memory tells me – and this is a story as much about memory as anything else – that I didn't think so at the time. I yearned for a vast potpourri of knowledge like the sea, stewing and spilling with wonders. Instead all was presented in an inland, linear mode that positively failed to capture my attention. You look as though you may have shared my disaffection.

There are star gazers and starfish gazers, and I am among

the latter. I would rather paddle and puff round a coral reef than touch the outskirts of the furthest sun. There's no right or wrong about these things, just a sympathy. Yet even as we agree, how we conspire! Our tolerance is negated by the sly superiority in our faces. Those who favour space have their own tolerant masks on, hiding their cosmic superiority.

At any rate, this predilection for the sea determined the course of my life, for better or worse. Impossible to say until the course is run. My romantic love for the tragic whale no doubt spared me other gravity-dominated obsessions. But that can only be speculation. At any rate, I had two great experiences of and from the sea, and it is those which I wish to relate.

My life moved inland for a time. An elderly relative was dying rather like a great, beached whale, after a lifetime of glamour and applause on high seas of success as a concert pianist. I felt I could not let her die alone. No doubt it was her resemblance to a whale that purchased my compassion.

At the same time, I was attached to a person, romantically attached, that is. I was spared only the most tempestuous excesses, not the entirety of folly. This person was a wanderer of the sands, a beachbum, as you Americans would say. It will be noted that I was looking at the social role or professional occupation of my lover, rather than directly at the individual. It is a common mistake, usually made in cases where both are rather more conventional. But it can happen in any case. Poverty and originality are no defence against romantic inflation, alas.

I was engaged in nursing the old doyenne of the concert halls, who looked incredibly shrunken and pathetic without her piano, like a hermit crab searching in vain for a home. She was dying slowly, which made the rest of the family clamorously impatient, but not me. She didn't know how to die, not having practised it beforehand, like her music. She was sight-reading, even composing.

She became possessed of the delusion that we were on board a ship, rather than in her rather fine country house. We were aboard together, bound for somewhere known to us both but also obscure by its very nature. When we arrived at our destination, she would disembark, I remain aboard. There was more than a little method in her madness. She had found a metaphor for the unravelling of her life. She told herself a story about what was happening to her and thereby alleviated her panic, her sense of helplessness. She had great presence and dignity as she lay alternately on the decks of her ship or within her rather queenly cabin. Meanwhile, of course, she travelled slowly but surely towards death, the port of call at which she would abandon ship and I would sail on without her.

Before she died, my beachcomber friend came to visit. He failed to comprehend the nature of her metaphor, which surprised me. I expected it to be just up his stream. I had misjudged him. I felt foolish, embarrassed and wary. I had been far more deluded than my poor old aunt, bravely ploughing the waves at ninety. I had assumed that we were soul-mates. We were no such thing. There was a prime, unresolvable difference between us. He was a real bum, one with no destination. Though I couldn't state mine, I was a celestial navigator of the seabed. I was searching, not just window-shopping round the coral reef, though I could not have said what for. He was a nomad, another breed altogether.

I sat with my aunt and wondered how best it could end. Neither of us was right or wrong. He was a vegetarian who ate fish. I should have known the truth from that, if nothing else. It must end without bitterness or blame, I fretted. I should have saved myself the trouble. We had loved one another and the love held true to the end. There were signs he could read, even if he couldn't come aboard my ship. He was not blind.

My aunt went to bed. We walked around the house on a sort of tour. Then we went to bed and made love. He slept soundly. I got up, restless and worried, and went downstairs to drink some water and to finger the shell he'd brought me as a present. I loved his beachcomber presents. This shell, though in no sense a bribe, was alluring. It provoked regrets in me, and a weakening of my resolve. It was then that I had my first revelatory experience of the sea.

The shell was gone. I had left it on the kitchen table, I remembered most clearly. It was absurd to think my aunt had touched it. She was anchored for the night. Panic rose in me.

The precarious nature of my relationship with the beach-comber made me founder in superstition. I would find the shell smashed on the floor, harbinger of our love's inevitable finale. Then I turned slightly towards the door, and I saw it.

I will never know how it left the table without shattering. Did it bounce like a tiny rubber ball? Did it parachute, or sprout tiny wings and waft down amid the chair legs? I don't know, and can't know.

All I know is that once it got down, it simply scrambled away to the crack in the door on its little spidery legs. There was a hermit crab inside the shell, unknown to both of us. I carried it upstairs like a baby in a carrycot and woke the beachcomber. He understood. He pocketed the crab and was gone by dawn, heading for the sea to throw the thing back. We had both shed some sea water from our eyes.

The sign, like all signs, was ambiguous, there for us to interpret. The crab was not dictating that we part, merely suggesting we separately pick up our beds and walk, for all that we had shared a bed. In our case, it meant an end. In any case, it would have meant separateness. It was a sign of an inveterate solitude.

Soon afterwards, my aunt reached her destination. She left me the house, and I did what seemed to me best with it. I sold it and used the money to book myself a passage on the

Watercress. I had saved every picture they printed of her while my aunt was dying. And there were plenty of snails in her neglected garden to remind me.

The ship was exactly as I'd dreamed. It was a mirror-image of the house. It had been essential for me to get off that ship after all, as if it could have only one destination, standing as it did in dreaded dry-dock. I needed to get my sea legs back again.

Once we got out into the middle of the sea, calm and waxy as it was, something began to follow us. We'd had dolphins challenging us before, but the captain let them win, which I thought was very wrong of him, and they must have thought so too, for they eventually stopped bothering.

There was nothing out here but the hot wax of the sun sealing letters, pages and pages of onion-skin waves. From God? Then this whatever-it-was trailed us.

It was torture. We superstitiously forebore to swim in the ship's tin-bath-like little pool. We stood at the railings instead and watched the thing. The others were certain it was a shark. I said nothing. What could I say? Yet the thing pulled at me like a magnet. I longed to plunge in and have it over with, but I distrusted my own instinct. I feared it was morbid. The crew were certain it was a deadly thing. It was dark, an ink blot on the water. If they saw death in it and I saw something else, didn't that merely reflect our differing perspectives, as such abstractions always did? I went round and round such arguments in my mind until it seemed to me the thing must be evil, simply because it had the power to drive me mad. I began to wish for the journey to be over, to plan a landlubber's life for myself once we docked. If we docked. The thing had thrown a shadow over my mind. Or was I projecting a shadow of my own over the water?

I was restless and insomniac for the first time, at sea. I paced the decks, always angling for a better view of the black thing. I tormented myself with regrets. Why had I sold the house? I could have lived there. Had I kept it and rented it, the beachcomber and I could have eked out a living. He, too, had come to pound the beaches of my dreams. I might even have learned to eat fish! I had gone wrong. I was cast upon the waters, homeless, with only this inky shadow for company, this malign unknown, like a dire future. I began to hate it, to wish to see it destroyed.

Everyone, in varying degrees, shared my hatred, my desire for bloodshed. Our black apostle must be dealt with. It floated ever closer. We felt foolish, helpless, allowing it to follow us with impunity. So had my aunt no doubt felt about death, until she decided to change course and pursue it, albeit at a measured pace.

We led it into port. Huge, tattooed sailors rowed out to us with harpoons and knives. The thing followed us right in, relentless, or oblivious.

Just before they hammered it with their blades, I had a passionate urge to stop them, a powerful sense of being aboard a nightmare. I said and did nothing. It's extremely doubtful whether I could have intervened effectively at that point. I might have provided myself with some comfort in the aftermath of what followed, but even that is doubtful.

It was a whale, of course, a baby whose mother had been felled by a whaler. In a flattering but fatal instance of mistaken identity, it had taken us for her, and followed us.

Ruth stopped, her voice wobbling. The two men blinked, and at the same instant a light bulged on, it seemed, from the wall, and a siren screamed, as if in protest at the slaughter of the baby whale.

✆ India's Tale

Once upon a time there was a child called Gloria Mundy. She was indeed a glorious, glowing, ginger child. There was something secretive about her as there often is about ginger people, something elusive. This gingerwoman quality made her all the more alluring. Even as a child she was alluring, but she responded to only one stimulus, like a secret vice, a guilty pleasure. Only her parents knew the source of her slightly cunning, foxy look, knew that it was different from the cunning, foxy looks that other ginger people wore.

Gloria was born with a red, bushy tail. They had it surgically removed, of course, but it promptly grew back. For a time they kept taking her back to the GP each time it replaced itself, redder and bushier than ever. Finally the GP suggested that as surgery seemed to encourage it, they had better try ignoring it and see whether that might have the opposite effect.

So they stopped taking her to the doctor. They stopped taking her anywhere. They hid her away, and themselves with her. The Mundy household became a silent, withdrawn, unhappy place. The Mundy parents felt that their strange daughter had robbed them of happiness. Of course the theft was involuntary, a sort of kleptomania. They kept giving her reassuring parental smiles in which their teeth were conspicuously prominent.

Gloria felt in turn that they were robbing her of happiness. Their smiles were the most relentless blackmail. It was a sulky *ménage à trois*, with a foetid, resentful atmosphere. They were all frequently ill with boring, mundane illnesses, flus and grippes and colds.

One morning as they snuffled and sniffled over the breakfast bowls, Mrs Mundy looked from her husband to her daughter, broke out in a cold sweat, and threw up.

'On an empty stomach, Mum?' Gloria asked.

'It wasn't food I was trying to get rid of,' Mrs Mundy replied with dignity. 'I was trying to rid myself of this house that sits like a rock cake in my gullet, of the life lived in this house that sits like a petrified raisin on the rock cake.'

'Oh, dear,' Mr Mundy demurred.

'Because thou art neither hot nor cold I will puke thee from my mouth,' she shrieked at him. 'That's in the Bible.'

'Such a literal mind you have, dear,' he shook his head.

'Literal,' she screeched. 'This child –' taking Gloria by the hand – 'this child has a *literal* tail. It's time we started facing facts. And helped her to take pride.'

He disapproved. She disagreed. Gloria wept. But Mrs Mundy held firm. They could hide the tail, they could hide behind the tail no more. It was time for the tail to come out. She took out her sewing machine and began working on a glorious new wardrobe of clothes with portholes, as she called them.

Gloria sulked. But she had to admit the clothes were beautiful. She had never had pretty clothes before. They were a bribe of sorts, an effective one. Gloria sighed over the portholes and trembled at the attention she was bound to attract. But the time had come to make her debut.

She began to have a relationship with the tail. Before, her feelings towards it had been limited to shame and fear of detection. Now she wanted to familiarize herself with it before she exposed it to the world's scrutiny. She looked at it. She stroked it. She talked to it. Being pubescent, susceptible and lonely, she fell in love with it.

The admission of the tail into society had a dramatic impact on the social status of the Mundy family. Gloria was assumed to be the product and victim of bestiality between Mrs Mundy and a member of the animal kingdom, un-identified except for the fact that it had a tail.

In an unguarded moment, she said that an orangoutang had been her downfall. She was believed.

Mr Mundy took it all very badly, or very well, depending on your point of view. He took it with the logic of the borderline insane. Mrs Mundy has confessed to consorting with an orangoutang. She could not be unfaithful to him. His scheme of reality did not allow for such a contingency. Therefore he, Mr Mundy, must be the orangoutang.

The borderline was trampled like a flowerbed. Mr Mundy was certifiably demented and duly certified. As far as he was concerned, he was incarcerated in a zoo. Mrs Mundy came to see him every day. She preferred him as a crazed orangoutang. She even suspected him of doing a St Joseph to protect her. But he was so convincing she thought he must be convinced. She enjoyed feeding him through the bars and having her fingers nibbled. As time went on they progressed to other intimacies which the wide vertical bars allowed and even enhanced. They were very happy for a time.

Meanwhile, Gloria began writing love poetry to her tail. Her love was unrequited, even unrequitable. Her poems languished unread, even unreadable. Her muse enjoyed the perfect lyric climate. The harvest would be opulent. She would be noted for the mysterious quality of her verse. Who was the gingerman – or woman – of her sonnets? Or had she perchance fallen prey to the family curse? Who or what was the gingery beloved of Gloria Mundy?

Only her mother knew. Only her mother knew, partly because such is the nature of motherly insight and empathy, and also because her father was, as it were, permanently out to lunch, for which he usually had bananas.

The tail matured. It grew and twinkled with gingery light. It stood up, it swept like the train of a satin bridal gown (but red satin, with mica-like sequins). It blew in the wind. It took raindrops like Christmas tree ornaments. It bobbed. It did everything, and a nice line in everything too. Gloria's poems began to beat with a fiercer, more contemporary plaint. They began to be the poems of a woman tormented by a strong, silent lover.

Then Mr Mundy, who seemed beyond the reach of change and destiny, suffered a reversal of fortune. The tail had become so beautiful, so decorative, with its lights and its style, dignity and buoyancy that everyone wanted one. Popular mythology demanded an alternative genealogy before the tail could be copied and mass-produced.

Mrs Mundy, so the revisionist history went, had been spectacularly modest. Mr Mundy was subject to the strains and stresses which inevitably fell on one in his lofty position. He was not an orangoutang. He was a demi-god.

Gods were out, but demi-gods were in. Every other person claimed to be one, and as the powers and privileges of a demi-god were rather obscure, no claim could be positively contradicted.

Soon Gloria didn't stand out in a crowd any more, except for the rather more persuasive lights given off by her tail.

The Mundys had failed to patent the tail, but Gloria's poetry boomed along with the tail business, so it really didn't matter.

Mr Mundy was given a private room in his hospital. He was pleased with his change of status. He was a conscientious sort of man, and he had tried his best to be a good orangoutang. It was very boring. This was much more fun.

110

He hypnotized his consultant psychiatrist, got hormone tablets off him, grew breasts and walked around the hospital chanting, 'I, Tiresias, have seen it all'. He was visited by suppliants who came to ask him to consider their problems. He was always glad to oblige. When his psychiatrist came to consult him about *his* problem, which was him, he suggested that he be sent home; and he was.

The Mundy house became a shrine. People came to consult Mr Mundy and stopped to hear Gloria read. Mrs Mundy ran errands, smiled with ever more prominent teeth, and muttered to herself. Where was her role in all this?

She began to be a quarrelsome, disruptive presence in the background. Her daughter was critically acclaimed. Her husband was uncritically acclaimed. Where did that leave her? She took to her bed for a week.

In the middle of the week, she was awakened from a half-comatose sulk by what sounded like a chuckle. It was mid-afternoon. The chuckle flooded the room as if the sun had laughed.

The next moment the sun was in bed with her.

'Don't be stupid,' she said to herself aloud. 'The sun's in the sky.' She went to her window to check. It was.

Yet there was another sun in her bed. She sat down and it began to radiate at her buttons. Remember, it beamed at her. Remember what?

Maybe it was just a cloud that had wandered in, lonely. But it was pink, flamingo pink, her favourite colour. Now she was flamingo pink. She was enveloped in the cloud. The cloud was deep in all her envelopes and pockets and seams. She was soaking with sweat. She rolled in the cloud, suddenly weightless. It seemed to pour into her like a syrup. She felt like a balloon filled with steam.

'How can a cloud climb in a window?' she giggled.

'Remember Zeus,' replied the voice. 'Showers of gold. That sort of thing.'

111

'You mean rape.'

'Do I?' The cloud asked, really rather tenderly.

'Well, no,' she confessed. 'But what on earth –'

'Who said earth? Nice place to visit but I wouldn't want to live here.

'I like the name Gloria,' the cloud said after a pause. 'Our daughter's name.

'Now do you remember?' The cloud spoke after another pause.

'It's dawning on me. I thought it was a dream.'

'It wasn't,' the cloud said smugly. 'It was me.'

'My husband is going to be very upset to find that he isn't the father of his child.'

The cloud shrugged. 'Why "father"? You assume there are no other forms of engendering than fathering or mothering?'

'I suppose I do.' Mrs Mundy cleared her throat. 'Are you a heavenly body?'

'What do you think?'

'Are you Mars?'

'Certainly not!'

'Uranus, then.'

'Don't be rude.'

'Do you have a name at all? Have you been discovered?'

'I most certainly have been discovered, and I have a name to prove it.'

'Which is?'

'Guess.'

'Don't tickle. All right. Is it a common name?'

'Certainly not. This could take forever, which is all right for me but not for you. Think of an event of galactic importance, of inter-galactic importance, that took place around the time Gloria sprung into existence, so to speak.'

'Eclipse?'

'The reverse, my dear,' came the soft response.

'Star – sun – moon –'

'Go back to star.'

'Twinkle, twinkle.'

'Big hint coming . . .'

'That tickles! Hair. Hairy star . . . comet. Halley's Comet! You're Halley's Comet.'

'Yes!' The comet hissed and wound round the room like a snake, picked her up and squeezed, but deliciously, without constricting. 'I am Halley's Comet, and Gloria is the child I made with you. I'm going to leave you a goldmine, all of your own. You can write your memoirs and make another one all your own, now that you know the truth.' The comet beamed.

'You want me to say what a great lover you are.'

'Of course I do.'

'So that when you come back –'

'Well, it will be a hundred years from now.'

'All right,' Mrs Mundy said tearfully. 'I'll do it as my memorial. And you'll remember me.'

'Oh, dear lady.'

'It's all right,' she waved the flash away like a camera that had snapped in front of her face. 'I can't escape my human destiny any more than you can escape your cosmic one.'

'Comic? But what makes you think –'

'Cosmic,' she shouted. 'Are all comets hard of hearing?'

She never knew. The comet was gone, leaving only the heap of gold in the middle of the bed. Tears twinkled in her eyes, somehow matching the smile that played around her lips.

Just then a siren blasted the bunker with noise, red lights and . . .

✑ Clare's Story

Some time ago I had to undergo a minor operation, minor in a dual sense of the word. It was a tonsillectomy that I required, something ordinarily endured in childhood when it may be uncomfortable, trying, even terrifying to a degree; but not, I assure you, the horrific trauma it becomes when performed on the mature. After the operation, I lost my voice. I felt far worse than that mean phrase communicates. I felt as if my voice had been amputated. I even heard it, as those who lose limbs are said to feel them in a phantom reconstruction. My voice was everywhere and nowhere. It existed only in my head.

My distress became extreme. I slept not at all. I seemed to hear my ghostly voice all the better at night, when all other voices were silent. I lay, moonlight striping my white hospital sheets, for I was moved to a private room, whether in my own interests or those of my fellow patients, listening, trying vainly to move my lips in tune with the sounds I heard, an arcane exercise that I can only describe as a ghostly inverse of lip-reading.

White on white, moonlight on crisp hospital cotton, changed daily (much to my distress, as I was used to enjoying a nest-like accumulation of crumbs, books, newspapers and other debris on my mattress at home), and the pale medium-like accompaniment of my detached voice – these were the colour-scheme of my anaemic hours. Friends came to visit me at first, then began to slacken the pace of their visits.

I lay on what I began to imagine was indeed my ice-floe and drifted into a stupor which might have led me into the ultimate silence, had it not been for Gemma.

Gemma was the woman next door. We had a doorstep relationship, which had all the subtle shadings such relationships hold if left alone to flower in their native habitat, and not brought inside to be bribed and tamed with tea or even with gin. They are a special sort of meeting and must be respected as such.

Gemma understood this. She tiptoed into my room, looking abashed, as if she half-expected the frost of my white, weary kingdom to chill her, too. I wept at the sight of her. My Beatrice had come, had brought me what I so desperately needed, a human voice rooted in a human throat and a human life.

We spoke a great deal about death. I was obsessed with it. Thanks to Gemma, I realised that I equated death with silence and hence had placed myself beyond the pale, as it were, from the moment my voice had fled. Half-seriously, using the pencil and paper which had replaced my phantom voice in her presence, I informed her that I had no intention of allowing myself to be booked into heaven, whatever my eventual fate. There were no animals in heaven, it was well known. Animals have no souls. Hence I would not suffer an eternity there.

She frowned. 'Surely you don't believe that,' she exclaimed. Before I could answer, she went on, and before I knew it, she had bidden me rise from my sickbed and follow her into another world indeed, not the one I had half-seriously anticipated, but the world of the story, which one must become a child to enter. I stretched out my hand as I closed my eyes, and we were off.

115

'Streets flowing with milk and honey,' she began, patiently. 'That indicates the presence of cows and bees for a start, does it not?'

I opened my eyes, thinking an answer was required. She nodded at me to close them again, and resumed.

'Anyway, I can tell you that there are animals in heaven, with the irrefutable evidence of an eyewitness. I have been there, you see.

'I, too, had dreaded the eventuality of heaven as it was presented to me. It sounded, quite simply, too white. A pale, gleaming, sterile place, rather like a modern kitchen without food or drink or mess of any sort, without a cat to brush your ankles, whining for food or purring like the casserole you lift the lid to sniff every few minutes for the sheer pleasure of it. White inimical textures, everything gleaming like tusks or formica, a synthetic gleam, an infinite pretence. The Emperor's new clothes come to life, but forever; for to protest against the glacial perfection of it, to fail to appreciate it, would be to mark yourself out as a sinner and not a saint. A conspiracy of silence, a unanimity of boredom in which misery lacked even company.

'I would protest. I would refuse and refute the empty glory. I would throw myself down and shriek with frustration. I would heave myself against the padded walls and keep up my tantrums until they were forced to remove me to the lakes of fire. There I would at least have warmth, light, colour and noise.

'I died. It was stupid of me, really. Not even an original death. I was quite livid with anger, which was advantageous to me in carrying out my plan. I arrived at the celestial gates determined to confront the concierge with my rage.

'To my immense astonishment, this personage turned out to be, not a self-important St Peter or an angel bristling with pin-feathers, but a great hairy ape amiably combing her armpits with a flashy comb set with what, in the circumstances, I could only assume to be real rubies. I was waved in with all the insouciance of a drugged parking-lot attendant, and in I went.

'Heaven, my dear friend, is entirely populated by animals. It is we humans who have no souls. Once you consider the proposition, it begins to make sense, doesn't it? Of course, you begin to mutter to yourself, of course! Another of those lies told according to the classical inverted design; like Adam's rib. Your brain is accustomed to simply turning the proposition presented on its head. This one simply slipped by undetected. Adam came head first from Eve's womb, where else? The first sin of our race was not the silly apple which she pushed on him in traditional maternal fashion, adding perhaps that it was good for him, would keep his bowels open, etc.; but the lie. Adam's lie. We are of course all sprung from the incestuous union of these two, something which, as Freud almost guessed, we all darkly suspect. As to the deleterious genetic effects of incest, well, that we must judge for ourselves.

'I correct my theology on one point: the sin is not the lie, but the envy that produces the lie. Adam envies his mother, and lies as a consequence. His pride will not permit him to drop (like an apple) from her womb; she must arrive from his rib. Is pride, then, the sin, or are pride and envy twins? Never mind. Enough scholasticism. We humans envy animals something they have which we have not; souls. Therefore we lie, and exclude them from our country club in the sky, our heaven.

'"But why," I ask the ape who admitted me, when she turns up again, "are there no people here?"

'"Oh," she beams in return, affectionately combing my cowlick, "we do hope you'll be the first to stay."

'With that she linked her arm through mine and skipped me away to tour the sanctuary.

'Others had come then, I mused, and gone away again. Was there perhaps a catch, some unpleasantness to evolve from the delight I saw and felt? I could only wait and see. It had also occurred to me that there might be some few advantages to be gained from my position as the only human being in heaven.

'The old notion of spellbound idleness crumbled before my eyes. Energy is eternal delight – and vice versa. Heaven was a place of bustle and change. It was the most creative place I had ever seen, a teeming hive of activity, all pursued – this was the secret – for its own sake, which is to say, for love. The very grapes grew for love, the wine fermented for love. I can hardly describe the sensation except to say that it was close, very close, to what happens on earth, with the sole difference of love. I cannot make it more exact or specific than that.

'Heaven is more down-to-earth than earth, that's the funny thing. Every action was practical, with a visionary practicality, without the impractical division we make on earth between work and play, between vision and realization. All such divisions had disappeared, and the memory of them was fading fast.

'The animals spent a good deal of time watching the planet earth with a sublimely compassionate, detached perplexity. They sent legions of guardian animals, of the sort we name dogs, cats, "domestic" breeds, downwards to try and help the human race. It was pitiful to witness the treatment meted out to these voluntarily mute creatures, who simply, silently, loved. Only the knowledge that they would be received back in paradise kept them going through successive abandonments, ill-treatments, deprivations and insults of all sorts.

'Sometimes they watched the antics of earth, nestling close to each other and chomping bits of fruit like children at a horror movie, squealing and hiding their eyes during the worst episodes. Sometimes they turned away from the spectacle and went to exorcise its ghastliness with a bath in a fresh spring or a session of gardening. Sometimes, of course, they sighed over human romance, or smiled over human joy. And sometimes they howled and hooted with laughter over the follies and fads of the human circus.

'How could we have assumed that God was of our species? Or of any species? I began, slowly, to understand certain things that had been murky before. Certain images came back to me. The Golden Calf, for instance. And half-digested bits of information; for example, the number of animals rescued from the flood, as opposed to the number of people . . . and: consider the lilies. Even plants could be held up to us as models.

'As, of course, they are. Buddhists come closer to recognizing their exemplars in the universe than we do. Only one thing was missing in heaven, with all the richness of the insight that began to come my way, to flood my being. I began to wonder whether it was the lack of that one thing that had driven others of my race from heaven's precincts. I could not share my craving with the animals. There was something that divided us irrevocably, after all. There were no books in heaven, not even Shakespeare or a Gideon Bible rattling around somewhere. I looked.

'Had I not stumbled upon a fatal flaw in the great design? I was intercepted while searching, blindly, for something I might read, and gently interrogated as to the cause of my agitation. When I explained, I was met with a smile. My tutor began to talk, somewhat irrelevantly I thought, about trees and paper, and the striking coincidence of the fact that human beings used these classicists, these poets, for raw material on which to produce their own works. Indeed, the animals had worked out that eventually all the millions of humans with typewriters might produce a living tree.

'Heaven was a library, an orchard of books. The trees were hung with fictions, inscribed on their leaves, all different but consistent to just the degree necessary to keep the warmth of familiarity. I could spend eternity curled up in a tree.

'But first I had further discoveries to make, far too many to list. Ostriches, for example, were mystics of the school and persuasion of Blake, whom they greatly admired (for animals, while on earth, devour the contents of our books without even opening the covers. They are engaged in so doing during the day, as they drowse or graze, as we think). Infinity in a grain of sand was their total preoccupation.

'Bats were the mother-figures of the upper air, forever offering their adorable little breasts. After much trepidation, I tasted this elixir and found it delicious, as was the sensation of being folded in the sable wings of a bat-mother, and listening to the vibrations of her singular lullabye.

'Rats were, of course, scientifically-minded, forever suggesting, tactfully, ways in which the human race might improve itself while allowing the humans to believe the ideas so presented were their own.

'I had thought to dominate this divine menagerie! Instead I fell into a stupor of depression and panic. How had I allowed myself to be so deceived? I was patted and fêted by my animal friends. Homesick, they sympathized. They understood.

'No, I protested. Homesick, for a place of degradation?

'I missed my friends, they suggested.

'Not a bit of it, I stoutly returned. On the contrary. Not one of my former acquaintances would, or could, comprehend what I now knew. I wished rather to relinquish my human skin, my human identity, to defect, as it were, to the better side.

'Yes, they said hurriedly, it was a temptation to which humans were prone, conversion, but –

'Not a temptation, I persisted. It was evolution. They looked somewhat embarrassed at this. A few of them turned aside to whistle or hum in their characteristic ways. I realized too late that evolution was not a notion that could appeal to them as anything but the supreme delusion of the human mind, in the circumstances.

'I apologised. I had decided, I continued, determined to make up for my error by making good my resolve, which species I wished to join.

'They looked up, silent; rather downcast, I thought. Then again, selection meant exclusion. If I joined one, I could not join all. Hence, perhaps, the rationale for their sorrow.

'I had settled on the zebra. There was no killing or being killed in heaven, I might add. Hunting was pure sport. Food was simply there, as I have explained. Meat was never missed; the taste for it had been extinguished from my palate. It had become unimaginable that one might ingest flesh. The prime disadvantage of zebrahood, then, was irrelevant here. On the other hand, they retained their air of delicacy, though no longer actually delicate of ankle or of heart. They preserved a slight air of graceful fragility, a faint air of invalidism, which would suit my bookish proclivities very well indeed.

'I presented my case with wit and brevity, or so I thought. My audience, by now sizeable, did not laugh when laughter was indicated. I thought I was demonstrating a praiseworthy honesty in describing my laziness. They frowned heavily, seemed distracted by some communal sorrow, which irritated me.

'I fell silent. Then I realized that the sadness in their faces was the sadness of farewell. We were parting.

'"What have I done," I exclaimed, "to be banished to hell?" For I presumed that was my destination.

'"You have banished yourself," they replied. "There is no hell except of your making, as you know, if you allow yourself to know; just as there is no heaven, except the one that you yourself create. You have made a hell by your betrayal of your own kind. You have lost your soul. All of you have lost your souls in this same manner." They shook their heads, baffled. "Not one of you has ever wished to return and attempt to instruct your fellows. Not one. There are no ghosts, no voices from beyond the grave, simply because no human has ever consented to become a ghost, to haunt a friend or relative with warnings or visions or greetings.

'"Now you must go," they finished. "Back, of course. To try to learn to love your own kind and so develop a soul. Good luck," they said. "You can do it," they said, trying to put confidence into their broken, defeated voices. "We shall be there to assist you, remember –"

'The orchestral insects played me out with a mock-triumphal piece meant to boost my spirits, but – '

'But' hung in the air as a bleep and a blast came from the machinery on the bunker wall.

✂ Curie's Story

It was a hot, close, claustrophobic night in the desert of disputed domain. The conflicting claims of the two tribes seemed themselves to clutter the air, crowded as it already was with insects and heat. The sands sizzled, then shifted as though boiling over into the air.

Miriam Guzman, one of an international team of archeologists at the site at some risk to life and limb, led by a thirsty curiosity that defied the glare of the desert and the threats of its predators alike, was awake this sultry night. She got up quietly, almost furtively, and wandered out into the area of the dig, or to its fringe. She felt it was unfair to venture into the freshly-dug sand itself. It belonged to the team. Yet it called her. It had called her before, that was why she was here. But this call was different.

She resisted it for a time, distracting herself with meditations on the nature and fate of the desert, the possible link between the two. The desert would be divided in two like the child brought before Solomon, she mused. Naturalists already decried the probable effects this would have on its flowerings, given the different uses the two tribes had for the land they would acquire. Precious, unique plants and

123

blossoms would be lost. Whole seasons which sprung into being under this particular sun would no longer occur.

Perhaps the desert has no real mother, she postulated. Perhaps it is the earth we should feel sorry for, the earth we call mother, herself so much in need of protection and nourishment. Who mothers her when we take to ourselves the prerogatives of perpetual childhood?

The moon was full. Perhaps that's why I can't sleep. She cast an eye towards the tents where her colleagues slept soundly enough, it appeared. But what was it that called? The moonlight seemed only a part of the summons, a beam fixed so that she might see in the darkness. Was it simply the spirit of place, of the empty desert itself, that had called to so many lonely spirits in the past?

Her feet were impelled towards the pit dug that day. It had an eerie, grave-like aspect in the moonlight. The moon made its own mirages, or so it seemed. Something trailed over the edge of the upturned sand. Something shone, or flickered. She went towards it like a sleepwalker. She knelt down at the edge of the pit, and reached towards the finger of light.

She felt a strange, light pressure, as if a grasshopper had leapt into her hand. So, she imagined, a child might stir in the womb. In her hand was a figure in crystal, a snug fit to the palm, unmistakeably rounded in the shape of an adult woman, indeed an old woman. How old, it was impossible to say.

She knelt cradling the tiny figure for immeasurable seconds, almost breathless with wonder and fear. She was terrified that it might die there in her palm, that she herself, by a sudden move, a violent jar, might be the cause of its collapse. She felt with all her archeologist's instinct that this embryo, or fossil, had travelled a long way to the harbour of her white, icy hand.

The figure began to move, to scratch. The crystal began to crack, and then to splinter, like an eggshell. She watched, afraid to interfere. How could she make herself in any way responsible for what was beyond her comprehension, even beyond her belief?

She sat back abruptly in the sand, just saving herself and her passenger from tumbling into the pit. She held in her hand the miniature figure of an old, walnut-skinned woman.

'Miriam,' the woman whispered sharply, and presented her hand. She saw her mistake immediately and withdrew it, looking somewhat discomfited.

'How did you know my name?'

'Your name? Miriam is my name,' rasped the ancient voice. Then the woman sighed. 'You probably know me as – Lot's wife.'

'Lot's – ' Miriam glanced towards the broken casing.

The woman nodded. 'Salt's a preservative,' she lisped. 'Especially to meat.' She let out a small but impressively worldly laugh. 'Well, what are you going to do? Eat me?'

'I'm not a cannibal,' Miriam said huffily.

'No,' the woman looked at her thoughtfully. 'Lucky for me we have the same name. Put me down, will you?'

Miriam gently obliged.

The woman walked over to the glittering fragments of her sodium shell, and forcibly kicked the largest of them away down the sand.

'That's better,' she said with a satisfied sniff. 'Well? What now?'

'What do you want to do now?'

'Do I have a choice?'

'Of course,' Miriam said softly, and waited.

'I'd rather not be a celebrity,' said the woman briskly. 'An intellectual sideshow freak. A curiosity.'

'No,' Miriam said, 'No, I can understand that.'

'A movie star,' the woman went on, 'a media star,' she shuddered. Then her eyes narrowed, and she looked up at Miriam shrewdly.

'Consider it carefully,' she said. 'All this –' her hand swept over the sand, the pit, the moonlight – 'could be

125

yours. In effect. You could be the greatest archaeologist of all time, if you brought me back, with this.' She booted another remnant of shell, then winced. She was only wearing sandals.

'But you'd be miserable.'

'Utterly. What's it to you? Go on, stand up and raise the alarm. You'll be worshipped, lionized beyond your wildest dreams, powerful beyond imagining.'

'What if I don't want to?'

'Don't want to what, succeed? Are you neurotic?'

'Don't want to hand you over, to betray you. To lose you, whatever you are. You might be more precious to me than all that, in some way I don't understand.'

'I might.' The woman smiled. 'Well? It's your choice. You can gain the entire world, or –'

'I'll take the "or".'

'Are you sure?'

Miriam nodded.

The woman closed her eyes.

After the silence had gone on for a minute or two, Miriam felt she might venture a question.

'What about – Sodom and Gomorrah,' she began hesitantly. 'If you don't mind talking about it.'

'Not now, I don't,' Miriam Two said bitterly, rocking herself back and forth as she spoke. 'The wickedness of it, the wickedness!'

'Wickedness – of the cities?'

Miriam Two shook her head fiercely. (It occurred to Miriam at this point that the other was Miriam One, beyond question, but she put the thought aside and stopped thinking in numbers.)

'Not their wickedness, not at all, oh dear no. They were experimenting, you see, they were ahead of their time, the peoples of Sodom and Gomorrah, and they were remembering, too, as people always do when they risk, when they experiment. They were remembering things they were supposed to forget, things that were inconvenient memories for those in charge, as memories so often are. Old gods, household gods, profusions of gods, not one mosaic God. That was very threatening to the order of things, as you may imagine. And then you see, they were gay and that, too, was perceived as a threat to the established order. Although it is still so perceived, I believe,' she went on sternly, 'with far less reason. We had reason to fear a dwindling of our population, as you do not. Which goes to show,' she went on avidly, 'that in neither case is it really to do with a pragmatic fear. In both, it is simply a fear of the unknown. Or, to be more precise,' she frowned in concentration, 'a fear of knowledge itself, whether carnal or spiritual. A fear of the intimate self, whether vested in intimacy with one's own sex, or with one's own gods. Do you see?'

Miriam nodded, somewhat dizzily.

'God was kept apart and aloof in the Holy of Holies, unmentionable except by initials, like a business tycoon. Not like the little household gods who were represented – also forbidden – and named, all the time. Sexual intimacy was surrounded by the ritual alienations of marriage, of differing roles – I should know,' she finished with a scowl, 'if anyone should.'

'But God destroyed them.'

'God,' she shouted, as best she could, indignantly. 'God! Do you actually think any God worth its salt, so to speak, would rain fire and brimstone on cities for a little sexual originality, or spiritual recovery? Come on, Miriam. Don't be so naive.'

'But then who –'

'The same ones who made up all the stories,' she said briskly. 'The rascals. The same ones who'll rain fire and brimstone the next time and blame the perverts and the atheists. It's always the same Lot – as it were.'

'But who turned you to salt?' Miriam burst out, unable to contain herself.

'You think I'm one of them, a know-it-all?' she fired back. 'All I know is, I was preserved for a purpose. I don't know what it is, I don't know how it was done. But I know enough,' she concluded.

'Why did you look back?'

She bowed her head, then lifted it and spoke very quietly. 'How could I not look back? Friends, kin, people who were part of me perished in the flames. Oh, I know it's conventional wisdom to flee, to *sauve qui peut*, to retire to your bunker and ward off intruders with a shotgun.'

There was a pause.

'But how could I?' The voice was a whisper. 'It wasn't even a question of what was right or wrong. It wasn't possible. I couldn't turn my back. Survival,' she shrugged, smiling sadly, 'is very important. But it isn't everything – or it wasn't for me. I didn't plan it that way. That was what happened.'

'The funny thing is, you did survive, in the end,' Miriam said shakily.

'Yes,' she whispered sombrely, 'that's the funny thing. Just as,' she went on, her voice gaining strength, 'you renounced a kind of survival just now, for something else – and that very survival, the success that you renounced, shall come to you through me.'

Miriam blinked. The partnership was sealed. Miriam the Elder led her to the blasted sites of Sodom and Gomorrah, which she revealed to the world along with their rewritten histories. They became the Promised Land of the gay community. Miriam and Miriam went on from there. The Elder had a nose like a pig for truffles for sites of indescribable significance and beauty, and she knew their biographies down to the last detail. She had instant recall for the deep past. The findings were controversial, hotly disputed in some quarters, always provocative.

'There are so many like me,' Miriam Elder sighed, before she died. 'Left behind by history without even a name of their own. Turned to salt because they know too much, because they refuse to forget. Someday they'll all come out of their shells.'

'Will they, Miriam?' the younger woman pleaded with her, 'will they? Will there have to be another cascade of fire first? Will –'

'I was only a prophet of the past,' her venerable friend replied. 'Not of the future, thank God.' Her eyes closed for the last time.

As if in response, lights flickered and flashed, sirens wailed.

℘ Davy's Story

Once upon a time there was a very famous photographer. Unfortunately fame made her restless and vain, as it can do, instead of gracious or grateful. Photography was a representational art, she reasoned. It did not originate reality, it merely reflected it. The same old mirror held up to nature, and nothing changed since Shakespeare's day. She wanted more than that.

She wanted to create, not re-create. She began to study alchemy. Her fascination began with a TV documentary about test tube babies, surrogate motherhood, the whole issue of reproductive technology and morality.

She brushed aside the moral problems. What gripped her was the sense of power behind the scientific achievements. God was overthrown, overridden, in the science of life, as He long had been in the science of death. God could produce earthquakes, floods and famines. They could produce oblivion in a blinding flash.

But now they had house-broken Eros as well as Thanatos. The photographer breathed envy and impatience at the TV. She began to expand her ambition, and her darkroom.

She had to subsidize her own research as well as to maintain herself in the inflated style to which she had long been accustomed, so she kept up her magazine work, which brought her into contact with great models of her day. They fascinated her. Each of them had a flaw, a blemish which she confessed to her photographer, her judge, with blushes and tremblings. These were meagre, microscopic faults, if faults they were. A crooked vertebrae in a wrist, an infinitesimally droopy earlobe, an imaginary blur or scar; these were their secret shame, the stuff of their private nightmares. These were the sins of the flesh they confided to her, hoping for the absolution of her airbrush.

She absolved them, but she blackmailed them in turn. She was not especially prepossessing in appearance, nor did she make the effort of personality to attract. She solicited sexual partners, for which she had a voracious appetite, by means of intimidation and blackmail.

She was thus assured of absolute discretion. Not, you understand, that she really had anything to fear from exposure. She hardly qualified as a lesbian, in truth. The women she sought were scarcely women. They were a concocted race, a hybrid flowering. That was the source of their attraction. In this she was like many men. Real women terrified her. She preferred the plastic princesses of the catwalks, those skeletal creatures who picked but never ate, let alone cooked, anything resembling real food, who looked at their own faces only in order to make them up, who never menstruated, thanks to international datelines.

She went through a phase of photographing prostitutes, but stopped abruptly. She couldn't blackmail them. Outside office hours they slept with whomever they liked, and they didn't like her. They had no use for the air brush. They lived quite happily with blemishes and flab. In some quite profound way they kept their pride. They could not be prostituted by anyone but themselves. They didn't sell their souls when they sold their flesh, at least not the admittedly up-market ones she photographed.

Pimps, on the other hand, were soulless. That revelation

131

might have spared her what followed, but she was beyond lessons. The exercise of photographing prostitutes puzzled her, and she disliked the sensation, any sensation, not immediately equivalent to omniscience. She abandoned the project, and returned to the models.

She began to tamper with them, not in her bedroom but in her darkroom. She began to subtly alter them, to improve or disfigure them as the mood took her. Her moods were arbitrary. Her sexual appetite dwindled; she was incorruptible. Nor did she keep her bargains and promises, when she made them. Why should she?

She was feared and hated. Models refused to work with her, at the risk of their careers. Hers was an era which made a cult of the sinister, which she epitomized. She was not only fashionable, she was Fashion.

But there was a fatal flaw in her system. The magazines that published her spreads, the manufacturers who published them, were less than pleased when she spoiled a feature by sabotaging the mannequin. The designers were furious. She could only get away with so much damage, which limited her power.

She needed magic, and she knew how to get it. She only hoped she had enough of a soul left to sell. She counted on the greed of the devils, and her calculation was correct.

She became known as the Dorian Gray of the Darkroom. Her magazine spreads were perfect. The models blossomed on the page, the glossy pictures betrayed unearthly beauty, breathtaking youth. The scars and birthmarks she etched into her negatives never appeared on the prints, only on the models' faces. Suddenly, wherever they happend to be at the time, they would feel odd volcanic sparks and clouds of smoke issuing around them. Then would come the eruption of wrinkles no facelift could smooth, of a single invincible wart on an aquiline nose, of a multitude of chins, a garageful of spare tyres no regime of diet and exercise could influence. Red stains appeared on the backs of priceless designer originals at their first showings, as women who had left their menstrual cycles behind them felt their careers engulfed along with their skirts in thick red seas that seemed to well up from the clothes themselves.

Then the tide began to turn. She had forgotten something. She had forgotten many things, ignored others. She had ignored the lesson of the pimps, who lost their souls while the women they robbed held onto theirs. She had forgotten that the thief always loses more than she gains, that she loses herself. She forgot that the devil is agent of confusion and plants her seeds in every pact. She forgot that the devil has no need to honour any bargain or promise.

Magazines began to dampen and shrivel on the stands, instead of selling out. People began to write articles and even books questioning the discrepancy between what was posed to them as 'beauty' in the pages of the glossies, and what they saw around them, and in their mirrors. They began to ridicule the classic features, streamlined shapes, fixed expressions of the models. They were ghastly anorexics with no more relation to human beings than the vampires they resembled. They preyed on the insecurities of women who bled and bred, with their impossible prescriptions of stainless, breastless, fleshless femininity. Why should women look like adolescent boys? Who were these mutants, dictating to the rest?

And what of the clothing designed for these fantasy creatures? What of the fantastic prices of the clothing? It was all a con. There was righteous indignation on all sides. Then alternative styles and prices began to develop that mocked and mimicked the old-fashioned stereotypes. It was all a joke, after all. The world rocked with laughter.

The photographer was courted for her ill-will, rather than for her favour. She had an uncanny knack of placing just that discrepancy, that quirk, that 'made' a face, according to the new canon. Those models who found they had

133

knifed themselves, surgically, out of the new market, begged for her curse.

She redoubled her efforts. She would not, could not learn. In this sense at least, it is absolutely correct to assert that evil is unimaginative. She could only perform more of the same 'evil'. She could not divert from her course. The wilder her distortions the more she revolutionized the notion of beauty, as applied to the human female. The side effects of this reform were quite extraordinary. Women were sturdier, stronger, bolder in every way, louder, surer. They hailed her, ironically, as their patron saint, their saviour.

She wept bitter tears. Finally she attacked her own self-portrait, thinking at least to profit from her own pyrrhic achievement. But her face remained its nondescript self. Only the photograph registered her vandalism. Again and again, she attempted to exploit her own fortune, with the same result.

She could change everything except herself. Such was the contract she had made with her diabolus. She had escaped the complaint of her race, that they could change only themselves. She had failed to observe that in changing themselves, they changed everything. She, in changing everything else, changed nothing.

There was an intense, theatrical silence, the accolade of silence that precedes applause. Then in place of applause, as the two men stood in tribute, their hands lifted as if in Papal salute, there came a clamour and a mechanical thunderclap, piercing, a din sufficient to wake the dead.

– and did it? Was the air filled with the yawns of the dead as they stretched? Were there pins and needles at the Resurrection?

Were the missiles fake? Did they spit big red flags with 'BANG' on them?

Did they turn into storks in mid-air and deliver babies instead of bombs?

Did the bunkers turn into gingerbread houses, the men into Hansels and Gretels, the women to witches?

Why, you ask, disgruntled by the silence, did the signals only go off at the *end* of the stories, thus stacking the odds against the women? Scheherazade always came to the good part at dawn, and stopped. That was her secret. Didn't they know that, and if the answer is 'realism', then how realistic is it for all the stories to end at the same time, when they're of various lengths, the last two notably shorter than the others? (And no bad thing, either, while we're on the subject.)

Were the women a) raped, and dragged off by the hair to begin the next civilization or b) killed?

Did the men die? Did one of them die?

Did the other man dance with the woman to a tune they

both heard in their heads at the same exact instant? Did they keep perfect time?

Were the men really women? Was one of them a woman? A Martian? A robot?

Were the women really elks, or big rocks?

Were the men really Greenham Peace Camp women who karate-chopped the Scheherazade women to the floor and laughed at their clothes?

Did all three of them peel down to red, white and blue satin jock straps and bathing suits and leap into the air?

Did they collide and knock each other unconscious?

Was there a *Deus ex Machina* in the missile system, installed by the Vatican?

Did it insure that everyone survived except:

    a. Homosexuals

    b. the Divorced

    c. Anyone who was having, ever had, or ever intended to have, sex, except

    d. With the express purpose of providing God with an opportunity to infuse another (poxy till baptism) soul into the world at the moment of ejaculation (which, if premature, carries a 999 day indulgence for mortifying the flesh of your partner)

What happens if the embryo is female?

    a. as far as we know, no infusion takes place, but if it does, it's probably temporary

    b. abortion is still forbidden, because it is forbidden to investigate the sex of an unborn child lest it be the cause of carnal pleasure outside Christian marriage, and also because any serious shortage of women to bear children would upset a lot of men in *very expensive* dresses.

Or – were the missiles the arrows that never arrive? Did they stay in the air, fracturing time but not severing it?

Are they there now?

Leave them. Leave them in suspended animation, paralyzed and dumb before the unimaginable. There is another story to be told, before the landscape is sufficient to their moment of truth. There are millions of stories to be told, to set the scene, their scene, in anything approaching its true perspective. I shall tell only one, or two; one which forks, as it must, to be complete. Perhaps it is an irresistible challenge to a storyteller, to take up another thread at the instant of peril, to burrow backwards just as the principals are stranded in time, aghast with suspense, and we with them. To provide the perspective in the only way I can, I must introduce you again to my mother Bee Fairchild, whom you have met in passing, and to my mother Lily Ghost, whom you have not.

Lily Ghost grew up on a caravan site. Her family was set apart from the others on the site, which was already a place set apart from the rest of the world. So Lily was doubly different, a cousin twice removed from the rest of her race.

The other children on the site were proud and wild. Their parents had chosen the nomadic way of life as a fierce privilege, or inherited it as a cherished tradition. Lack of schooling was a small price to pay for their election.

Lily went to school. The Ghosts were permanently planted on the South London site. They were not nomads. They lived in a caravan, not because they needed or valued mobility above all else, but because Michael Ghost was a ne'er-do-well and they had nowhere else to go.

He could charm the birds from the trees, but there were no trees on the site. Lily was taunted and teased for going off to school and taunted and teased when she got there. How did she get her post through the door, she was asked, when she lived somewhere without a road or a number?

It was a problem. Bridget Ghost made enquiries. The post came. It was mostly bills. The paper was delivered, which was considered the height of affectation by the others. They had the last laugh when it had to be cancelled.

Lily hated her parents for singling themselves out for such ridicule. She dreamed of normality the way some children dream of flying. If only they could be inconspicuous. But Big Mike's laugh boomed out, usually at himself, and Bridget talked to herself all day long, using a maternal 'we' that was a cross between a medical, royal and editorial usage. She made up for the newspaper, which she missed. She commented on everything, gave the world her opinion of it constantly, as if the world cared.

They gave Lily headaches. She wanted to tell them to shut up, or shoot them. But you couldn't do that, any more than you could huff or puff away the caravan. They were two feckless, engaging children, and Lily was hopelessly, bitterly in love with them.

She paid as little attention to this love as she could. Maybe it would go away. Meanwhile, she played outside the caravan, in the concrete yard. She lisped to her dolls, charming them in Mike's voice or chiding them in Bridget's. When it rained, she left her plump rubber dolls in their makeshift bed under her own bunk, and played with paper dolls. They were thinner, they took up less room, and there was little enough of that, stuck inside with Bridget on a rainy day.

Bridget had three more daughters before she had her tubes tied. Lily wasn't sure what that meant, only it made her mother cry just as she'd cried when the newspaper boy stopped delivering to the door.

'It's the possibilities I miss,' Bridget sighed as she tidied round the caravan, moving more slowly after her return from hospital. 'Just the possibilities, nothing more. Nothing can ever happen again, now.'

It must be like having your hair tied back in a pony tail, Lily surmised. It was all right like that, provided the rubber band wasn't too tight, which could suck back your cheeks and make you blink. But when it was untied it hung down

139

loose in the wind, it flowed right down your back. It felt alive, full of possibilities, like Bridget said. Your face felt fuller, too, and you could move it more. She wouldn't want her hair tied back forever, like Bridget's tubes.

'I'm gunner cut yer pony tail right off, in yer sleep,' threatened one of the boys on the site. She had nightmares about it for weeks, and pleaded with Bridget to let her sleep with her hair loose.

'It'll be an unholy mess in the morning,' Bridget sighed to herself. She only really spoke to herself, or to some nameless interlocutor only she could perceive.

'I'll brush it in the morning,' Lily said boldly. Bridget had always 'done' her hair of a morning. But her brushing lacked energy now, and the pony tail was often off-centre, slack, the hair itself lustreless.

'Might as well,' Bridget said to the cooker. 'Have enough to do.' She'd almost stopped using the pronoun 'I', ever since Mike rented a television set. It increased the claustrophobia of the caravan, for she kept it on all the time. Sometimes she fell asleep with it on, and Lily had to get up and switch off the stupid blank screen with its high mosquito whine.

She took charge of more than her hair. Mike was away more and more often. Lily simmered with resentment, but he reduced the place to chaos, knocking things over, drunk and disorderly, making them all laugh, when he was there. Laughter itself took up more space than they had, though at least it drowned out Bridget. She prattled along happily enough, as if things happened again with the TV on. Too much happened, Lily felt, in that small space.

Mike couldn't keep up the payments and the set went away. Bridget went around accusing the other women on the site of stealing it. Then she sat staring at the wall. Lily tried to persuade her to look out of the window.

'Like a blind person wearing glasses,' Bridget stormed at her. 'Just for the sake of appearances.'

Lily allowed to herself that Bridget was right. She was

140

often right in a hit-or-miss sort of way, with her songs and sayings and odd-angled observations.

Lily didn't have much time to listen. She did all the shopping, cooking and washing. Bridget still liked to fold things and iron, and Lily didn't like to impose too much on the younger girls. She herself was twelve.

The others began to find friends and footholds in the world outside, and Lily breathed more easily, literally and figuratively. They were less underfoot. At the same time she felt with a sinking feeling that she was marooned on a desert island with Bridget, who grew increasingly silent. When she was fourteen she got a Saturday job, and assuaged her guilt by renting another TV for Bridget. Mike ducked his head when he saw it, and smiled sadly at her. His hands shook, and even in the crowded caravan he seemed insubstantial, but it must have been the booze.

Lily felt shadowy, too, as if she had inherited missing links, negative rather than positive genes, from both her parents. It bothered her that her stomach sank inwards when she lay down on her bed, and her hipbones stuck out like the mastheads of a sunken ship. She felt sunken before she set sail, somehow. When she stood up there was more to her, her body rounded at least, if it didn't swell; but the sunkenness was still there, her secret shame or sorrow, like some kind of inverted, illegitimate pregnancy, an absence instead of a presence. Her notions of it were vague when she lay trying to frame them, or when they came upon her abruptly in the company or rather the presence of others. It was doubtful whether she ever put herself into their company. She had acquired a method in the caravan of being there but not there, and she kept it, a sort of shield or cloud of unknowing that would become an emotional cataract in time, unless something happened. She already knew this with the prescience of adolescence that sniffs the dangers along with the possibilities inherent in its own stuff. Sniffs, without identifying; Lily could not have said what she

141

knew, or used it to help herself. She could only feel the impact of the knowledge, the force of it.

The sense of something missing, some shameful absence, was bound up with sex, a sort of personal parallel to the different sexual secrets she sensed in others. She was utterly ignorant. Bridget had muttered a few tutelary remarks at the sink and left it at that, as if she believed that sexual information was disseminated by the wind, if not that sex itself was wind-dispatched.

Lily's guilts and persecutions tangled into tight, inextricable bunches. She felt guilty because there was no space, no privacy, in the caravan. These things drove her mad with humiliation and rage, yet it was as if she herself had created them. They had far-reaching consequences which made her guiltier still. Somewhere in the mists and miasmas of a sensitive, solitary conscience she believed Mike had fled in embarrassment bordering on horror from her developing body. That same body had driven Bridget mad. These self-accusations were never stated even in her mind, let alone clinically examined. They were just there, in sudden vertiginous moments that swept her away, like Elijah in his chariot.

In the meantime, school baptized her into print. She was born again, and again, between the pages of a book. Books masked her face and took her mind off its dim, troubling preoccupations. They even soothed her body, made it fade, temporarily. She had always read, bumping round the caravan with her nose in a book. Now in adolescence she read compulsively, as some girls ate. She felt starved without a book beside her, an alternative world to dive into whenever she had a moment. She read in the street, on her way to work, as she walked along.

'Careful, luv,' people warned, or they laughed at her, or they stared.

She didn't mind. She was finding herself as the girl behind the book. It was someone to be. It was a million masks, and one. She had a purpose in life now. It was to finish this book, and then the next.

'I used to read,' Mike said wistfully, disturbing her. She caught a glimpse of someone other than the greying delinquent man he had become. It hurt her to see him as he had once been and might have remained. It frightened her. The younger Mike had read books, like her. Could the later Lily ever be like him?

But the bond between them remained. Bridget saw it through her own sly obsessions with the ghosts of the TV, about whom she gossiped to herself constantly.

'Off to the library again, are ye,' she'd snarl at Lily. 'Dreaming yer life away, just like yer father.' She had found the sore spot, the soft spot, and she probed it, when she remembered.

Lily just looked at her, and slammed the door. One day the words in her mind would break through: at least he's not crazy. One day they did break through and she rushed back to the caravan from the library in a panic, expecting to find Bridget dead or just gone, gone, disintegrated by her cruel words. She was not, of course.

But the words had sunk in, just the same. Bridget took hold of Lily's suggestion. From that day on, she acted crazier. Lily had given her an option and she had taken it.

'I'm going,' Lily told Mike. 'I practically live in the library now as it is, along with the drunks.' He winced; she plunged on. 'I can't look after her any more.' She didn't say that sometimes she had surprised herself sitting in a church, any church, overcome with fits of weeping, that ministers of various sorts had approached her and offered counsel, that she had fled, appalled that her angry despair should overflow and become visible. She needed, at the very least, somewhere to cry.

Mike seemed to comprehend some of what she didn't say. He nodded and sighed, then he covered his face with his hands and looked out only to ask, thinly, 'Lily, Lily, what has happened to your mother?'

143

She got up and moved away to pack without answering. What answer could she give? Why had he asked her? She'd been offered a fulltime job in the shoe store where she worked on Saturday. She looked into the future and saw a narrow room lined with shoeboxes, smelling of feet and leather. She told herself she didn't care. There was the other, wider room, lined with books, smelling of paper. She could live between the two of them. The cover of a book was the door to *her* room, to her home.

She had to take the TV back. Bridget wept, then went silent. Lily felt as if she'd pulled the plug on her life support. But then Joan, who was fourteen, got herself a Saturday job, and the TV came back. Lily breathed more easily. Bridget was a basket case, but she was no longer carrying the basket. Now, maybe, something would happen.

This 'something' was another muddle, an expectation of change that was idealized and also sexual. Mostly it was undefined; apocalyptic, tragic, wonderful. Meanwhile, Lily answered ads until she found a flat-share, learned to operate a switchboard and landed a job in a West End office. She was quiet and respectable, and well-spoken, what with all her reading. Her voice was pleasant. She had found something she could do.

'Women, not girls,' one of her flat-mates sniffed when she first went to see them.

She supposed they were women. It had never occurred to her before. She went home weekly, then fortnightly. Bridget had become a muttering bundle who confused her daughters' names and thought Mike was the postman. She waited for the news that never came, she told Mike to go and find the errant paperboy. She sagged in her chair, watching the TV.

Lily heard her voice sometimes, among the disembodied voices on the switchboard. She forced herself to ignore it, and stopped going home. She took a typing course and was

144

given a rise. One of the other women left the flat, the one who had told Lily she was a woman, and she moved into her room, which was large and sunny, the senior room of the flat. She had status in her small world, a place.

But Bridget's voice still mumbled and sometimes made her confuse her plugs on the switchboard. Bridget huddled in the caravan. Lily began to huddle in her room. She rented herself a television with an eerie feeling of compulsion. She imagined that she and Bridget watched the same programmes, that they communicated through the grey, flickering images. Sometimes she left the TV on all night, and woke up grey and flickering herself.

One lunchtime, hunched over her sandwich at her desk, she saw one of the clerks go by with an armload of books. Books! She'd stopped reading since she left home. She got the location of the library from him, and started spending her lunch hours there. She felt restored. The TV was silent. She piled books on top of it.

She was called home for a counsel of war. Bridget was to be packed off to hospital. She was giggly and incontinent. The caravan reeked. Mike was selling it. They were scattering.

She kissed Bridget's cheek feeling like Judas. Not because she could prevent what was happening, but because of the sense she still harboured that somehow she had caused it by remote control. She had been on the upswing, therefore Bridget had to be down. It was a savage law, a primitive requirement for human sacrifice that stood between them. She might have offered herself, but she had not. She had sacrificed Bridget instead.

She visited Bridget. It was safer to see her in hospital than it had been at home. Bridget took her for a nurse, which gave her a sort of neutrality. She began to feel that she was a nurse, tht Bridget had made her one.

Bridget thought she was a dying gypsy woman. She wanted her caravan burnt, she told Lily, her nurse. Lily nodded. It would be done, she said with a baroque formality. They played a little scene between them whenever Lily visited.

Sometimes the scene changed. Lily was a nun who had taught Bridget when she was a child. Lily began to feel she was a nun. Bridget had made her one.

Mike sold the caravan, got a job in a pub and a room. He looked tidier than he'd looked in years.

'Should've got a pub job years ago,' he said cheerfully to Lily. 'Always too afraid of the demon drink. I'm actually drinking less now, with the stuff all around me.'

'That's good, Dad,' she was amused by his perversity. Her sisters rang her occasionally, as she did them. They were all waiting, as Bridget used to wait, for the news.

It came. Her funeral was a bleak affair. They gathered, sombre and secretive as conspirators. Their conspiracy, their family, was over. There were no more phone calls. Lily lost track of her sisters. They were engaged, married, they had children. Mike's voice boomed over the phone, telling her. And what was she up to?

She met people, and told them she was an ex-nun, or an ex-nurse, whichever she thought they'd prefer. She wore black. People thought it was interesting, that she was called Lily, and always wore black, and had a history. Only she knew that nothing had happened. Then she saw an ad in a newsagent's window, and something did happen, at last.

GUARDIAN ANGEL wanted for BABY WOMAN,
mother at Greenham Peace Camp, close 3-way relationship,
correspondence

'I had to look up "correspondence", to see which sort,' Bee
confessed over tea. 'It's like stationary, or –'

'Sanitarium,' Lily supplied. She shone, metamorphosed
by her signal luck, or grace. She had found her place. She
had known it immediately. She could hardly keep her eyes
off Curie, the BABY WOMAN of the ad. She was eighteen
months old, hardly a baby at all, mobile and charming. And
charmed; she toiled over and pulled at Lily for a hoist into
her lap.

'She likes you,' Bee said with satisfaction and relief. 'It was
all right for her when she was smaller,' she went on again,
still listening to her own story to see if she believed it, 'at the
camp. But now she needs space to move in, and I do still
have the flat –'

Lily nodded, hiding her face in Curie's hair. She was to
move in and look after Curie, keep the flat, write to Bee.
That was the correspondence. Even that part enchanted
her. She sensed she had a chance to make something of a
friendship located and conducted on paper. And as for

147

Curie, well, the friendship was there. She felt like Pharoah's daughter, she told herself with her old, inflated, Biblical sense of events. She had found a child, a daughter, in the rushes, on an ordinary morning, and now nothing would ever be the same again. She hugged Curie close and then let her clamber down in search of cake.

'And you're a nurse, too,' Bee said appreciatively. 'Not that that's essential, of course. But it can't hurt, can it,' she laughed with pleasure at this excess of rightness, of justification. 'What a full life you've led, first a nun and then a nurse,' she observed respectfully, almost enviously.

Lily nodded gravely. 'Indeed,' she intoned, and quietly went over in her mind the hospital background and training she had filled in for Bee, making it up as she went along. She was good at that, and she enjoyed the sense of risk and adventure it gave her. It was sometimes hard to remember it afterwards, that was all. She would have to develop the nun, some time, to give her another chance to show off her virtuosity, to herself of course. Other people had other ways of showing off to themselves, of preening. She watched them do it. Well, this was her way. The almost physical place where she located her most private thrill was the imagination. Was there anything wrong with that? She was wriggling, now on her chair, already hearing herself shyly confessing to Mike someday that she, too, had a child, an unsuspected daughter. She would present him with a grandchild. He would visit. Someday. She turned her attention back to Bee.

'Lily Ghost, what an interesting name,' Bee had murmured when they shook hands. 'It is your – real name – I suppose?'

'Yes,' Lily nodded, surprised to find herself telling the truth, almost by accident. Bee had doubted that one, absolute, unvarnished fact, and swallowed all the rest without a murmur. It was a gleeful irony somewhere inside her. Eventually she would embellish the bare outlines of her convent career, describe her crisis of faith, her wrenching departure. She knew it would go over well. She had gauged her audience. The wide blue eyes under the shock of blonde hair were hers, a captive audience and a receptive one.

Then there was the other pair of eyes, Curie's, so alike and so different. More slanted and bluer, too, Siamese cat-like eyes. A cast to the face that made you wonder where she came from. Her father was Chinese, Bee said. She laughed and said she liked Oriental men and Occidental women, and did Lily think that was racist, or sexist, or what?

Lily just shook her head. She had no idea. She had lost her own virginity to a librarian in a brief, rather brutal episode. He had brought no skill of any sort, sexual or social, to the interval, for that was how she thought of it, rather than in Bee's word, as a 'relationship'. It was an interval, an accident, and it left her with a permanent effect, like a dent in her fender. That was all. Needless to say, she had had no skill either. Books were no help whatsoever, she found to her great disappointment. She had changed libraries, as a way of misplacing her lover.

Lily might need a tissue of lies like a protective membrane between herself and Bee. But nothing would come between herself and Curie. They would have a 'relationship'.

She arranged with Bee that she would move in the following week, after she 'wound up her affairs', as she said, falling back on formality.

Bee had looked at her and laughed. 'If you want to have people in, do,' she said vaguely. 'Only if you have someone living here –'

Lily's head was shaking vigorously. 'I'm not like that,' she said tartly. 'The little one and I will live together, thank you very much.'

Bee nodded, looking slightly abashed.

Lily got outside, feeling that she had made exactly the right impression, a sort of Mary Poppins figure, a bit eccentric but all the better for that. And the nursing, that clinched it. As for her 'affairs'! As if there were anything to wind up. Well, there was the flat, she supposed.

She stopped off at a bookshop with the unique errand of buying a book for Curie. Funny name. Wanted something different, Bee said, something strong. Shaking her head, Lily went insid. Never mind. She'd give her the best gift there was, she'd teach her to read. But first she'd read to her. That would be a gift to both of them. She still couldn't credit her luck. One day she was bored with her job, stale and lonely, hating the trivial relationships she endured with her flatmates, all brightness and lies. *They* were the lies, those poisonous smiles in the kitchen that took away your appetite. Not her stories. They were different.

'For my niece,' she said to the woman at the cash desk as she paid for the book. The woman smiled in acknowledgement that aunts had status and presence and place in the world, and Lily left trembling. To Bee she was a nurse-turned-nanny, to Mike she meant to be a brave single mother, and now she was an aunt to the woman at the cash desk. Where had that gratuitous lie come from? She opened her mouth, and there it was. One of the family, literally.

She stopped to stare down at a train plummeting along on the line beneath her. Lies were like that, carrying you along towards somewhere, towards something. At least you weren't standing still. 'Possibilities,' she heard Bridget sigh and turned as if she expected to see her there at the railway bridge, at her elbow. 'Possibilities,' she sighed again, and was gone.

That's what Bridget was after. Possibilities. That's what I'm after, with my stories. Lily walked on. Bridget wasn't as firmly buried, as forgotten, as she'd thought.

Well, she'd be what she was, to Curie: a storyteller. Let there be that truth between them. Her eyes glowed in the dusk just thinking of the child.

Her flatmates made her a farewell dinner. They all drank

150

a lot of wine, and ended up watching television, talking to each other through the flickering pictures. Lily shivered, thinking of Bridget. There was no TV in Bee's flat, she'd noticed, and relayed her approval.

'Oh, I'm so glad you're not an addict,' Bee said warmly. 'I couldn't have anyone around who watched it all the time. It'd be so bad for Curie.'

Lily fervently agreed. She felt safer without a set on the premises, further removed from the ghost, not so much of Bridget herself as of her madness, her monologues, the fixed concentration and almost clownish bafflement with which she'd watched the miniature people on the screen, like an animal watching humans.

She packed the day after the party. The entirety of her material possessions fitted into four tea chests. She called a taxi, which made her feel like someone in another life, an effective, active life. But then, she reminded herself as the taxi coughed away, she was someone else from now on, and her life was both active and effective. It amazed her to think, as they swept through the streets, she was suddenly someone the people on the pavement might possibly envy. She had things not a few people might covet; a nice place to live, a child to live with and care for, a friend. She had never had so much before. She was like someone in a book. The page turned, the chapter ended. On the next page, in the next chapter, fate smiled. Everything changed. It had happened to her.

She arrived dazed and blinking. What would the next page be like, and the next chapter?

Dear Bee,

Today we went to the park. Fed the ducks. Curie wanted to dive right in with them, I had to hold her by the back of her jumper, a new jumble sale one from the church on the corner. They saw us passing and one of the women came up and asked if she could use it. She chatted away to them in her own language, the way she does, for a quarter of an hour. You meet a lot of people, walking around with Curie. The jumper's blue, it does suit her, and it was lucky she had it, leaning over the ducks.

We took a picnic lunch, it was blowy and fresh and she doesn't mind the cold, she keeps on the move, so do I behind her. She'll talk to anyone without the slightest fear. Makes me tremble sometimes but I don't want to put her off, the way we talked about. The only way is to stay right behind, close, and keep a good watch.

She loves the launderette, no use you worrying about not having a washing machine. She'd be ever so upset if we didn't take the clothes along in the trolley. She likes to help, it makes for a longer morning, but what's time for if not that? Then it's lunch and a nap. She always sleeps soundly after the launderette. It's all the excitement I suppose.

Lily paused, smiling over the paper. All the excitement of the launderette! The odd thing was, the excitement communicated itself. It passed through everyone who came within Curie's range. She made the dingy shoebox-shaped launderette with its floorful of cigarette butts and grey soap powder into another realm. It was not the sordid place Lily had once spent whole weekends avoiding. She made it a party, toddling back and forth from the machine to Lily to give her vivid bulletins, or proudly carrying damp clothes to the dryer, holding them up over her head to keep them away from the ashy floor. Lily found she forgot the book in her lap and watched Curie unfold before her eyes. She made the world new for Lily, with a newness more immediate and continuous than the revelation of books.

Tears tingled behind Lily's eyes as she wrote. The tingling was becoming familiar. She had never cried so much before, or at least not so easily. The fits of weeping that had driven her into churches in the past were violent and frightening. She had sought sanctuary from them. But these tears were gentle, bittersweet expressions of a fullness of life that rose up in her and overflowed. She laughed with Curie, and when Curie slept she cried, more often than not.

She straightened in the kitchen chair. She had to concentrate. She had something to say to Bee. It had come to her that she must do something for Curie, something that would otherwise be left undone.

> There's something on my mind. I know we both have a sort of religious background in common, not exactly the same one, but we're both what you could call broadminded, you don't hold with what your family thought about papists and I know there's more to the Church of England than my mother used to say, that it was built on the balls of Henry VIII.
>
> So but there is still one problem and that is Curie. I know we have both come a long way from the Pope and the balls (!) but it's important not to throw out the baby with the bath water. And it's come to me, watching her, and watching the washing go round in the machine, it's come to me that she should be washed clean too, not as they say in the blood of the lamb or anything horrible, just as a natural sort of welcome and protection. And not by some scaly priest in a dark church,

153

mind. But I remember anyone can baptise in an emergency and I reckon that this is an emergency, just like you do, with the missiles all ready to go off to Russia any moment Ronald MacDonald decides. So I would like to do it. Just in case.

I hope you are all ok there, I read about you in the paper every day and think about how brave you are and try to tell Curie. I think she understands a little. There's a sketch of some ducks on the back – I'm telling you just so you'll know what it's meant to be, with lots of love from us both

Lily Ghost

She addressed the envelope in her firm, flowery hand. She belonged in the world now, not only by the grace of Curie but also by the presence and purpose of Bee and her friends, some of whom usually contributed a line or a cartoon to Bee's letters. Lily's circle had grown wider and wider. For the first time in her life, she was even connected to things that went on in the newspapers. She saw the name 'Greenham Common' and heard it on the lips of people around her. She was part of it.

But why this archaic instinct to baptize Curie? Lily sighed. She didn't know why, really, but it was there. It nagged at her. She re-read her letter proudly. It was something, to be able to spell and make sentences. It was something she had taught herself. No one had bothered a lot with her, at school. They seemed surprised by her written work, and suspicious, as if they thought she'd copied and cheated even when it was transparently clear that she couldn't have done. She resented their astonishment, and the tactlessness with which it was expressed. Bee was not surprised. She took Lily at face value and expected the best of her.

The argument about the bomb was a heartfelt one. It had never meant anything to her before. Now it did. Now there was an urgency about it because Curie's life hung in the balance, but also because Lily's own life, linked to Curie's, was a life worth saving. She was afraid of losing what she had so recently found, which was everything. The notion of

154

baptizing Curie was a sop to the gods, an attempt to appease their probable jealousy and keep their wrath at bay. If she made a serious symbolic offering of what she loved most, perhaps she would be permitted to keep it.

Also, she mused, baptism wiped away all accrued sins, all due punishment. She remembered her catechism. Bridget and Mike had sent their daughters to Catholic school. Curie had no real sins. Original sin didn't count. Would not God, in the economy of salvation, apply the general pardon of the sacrament to Lily? Might she not be granted a fresh spiritual start, just as she had been granted a physical and an emotional one? She felt certain that this would be so. Her faith was a strange mixture of superstition and logic, its spirit mostly culled from Bridget's lore.

Lily chewed the end of her pen and calculated Jesuitically. There was the case of the Emperor Constantine. He had himself baptized on his deathbed. A ticket to heaven. Of course, he took the risk that he might die unexpectedly. But he had a good Guardian Angel, it seemed. He had survived to receive the sacrament, which made him a saint in spite of everything that had gone before, though they never had got round to canonizing him.

Lucky. Could have been caught with his pants down. She chuckled to herself. Her inner life had become increasingly ribald since she'd been in contact with Bee and her friends. Their language was sharply sexual and rich, with it. She had adopted it in her head, if not yet in actual speech. The Greenham women brought an atmosphere strangely familiar when they came for weekends. It was like the atmosphere of the caravan in the weeks and months of Mike's many absences, she realized, but different. Instead of ever-increasing sense of danger and helplessness that had haunted the Ghost household, with ever-diminishing Bridget at its helm, there was an opposite sense here of power, of *possibility*, that which Bridget had so craved. It existed, outside books.

155

She thought of her sisters. For all she knew, they could be different now, too. After all, they had children. They had left the sad, scared years behind. She would contact them through Mike. First, she would have the satisfaction of presenting him with his grandchild, Curie. She rose from her chair and went to look out of the kitchen window at the pale suburban road. There was something missing in her Firm Purpose of Amendment, when she was already planning another lie. It had worked for Constantine, but he had died immediately after the baptism, with no time to sin. He'd have had no time or energy for so much as an impure thought to consign him to purgatory. Or had he cursed or lied or something, at the end? Was that why he was never canonized? She thought of Thomas something or other, a martyr who was buried alive. When they dug him up to see whether he was preserved from corruption in the Odour of Sanctity, they found that he'd scrabbled and bitten at the cloth inside his coffin. They couldn't make him a saint, in case he had sinned at the end by despair.

She brought her mind back. After the baptism, Curie would be her godchild, and so in a sense related to Mike as well. God would understand, as he must have understood the clawed and chewed coffin-lining, whatever they said. If He didn't, there was Bridget to plead for her. She'd argue with God till he agreed, just to shut her up. There was no doubt she was in heaven. All mad people were.

She made the sign of the cross over the letter and sealed it. If there was hypocrisy, even opportunism, in her newfound faith, well, she was only human. She felt secure from all censure now. Just one more lie to set the final seal on her new life, to legitimize it, and all would be well. That sense of absence that had haunted her in adolescence would dissolve. As a mother, she would finally be safe.

Bee wrote back immediately, agreeing. Her friends added their endorsements. They all wanted to be part of the ceremony. This baptism would be unique. They would

156

welcome Curie to the community of women, with Lily officiating. They would have another ceremony, of confirmation, when she had her first period.

Lily blushed. They would see it like that. But it didn't matter. She sighed with satisfaction and relief. They hadn't even mentioned her ex-nun or nurse-ship as qualifying steps for this ultimate office. They seemed to assume it was hers for the asking. Maybe the lies didn't matter so much. She had suffered so, agonized over the unlikely event of exposure, the bare fact of fraudulence. But she was loved, it seemed, for her Lilyness, which the fraudulence and the agony were part of, though they didn't know it. She wept over their love and their ignorance, and over the difference the letter made to her plans. She had pictured a special private audience with God for her and Curie. But the women had different ideas. They wrote that baptism was a rite of passage and it should be saved till Curie could participate more consciously. They would wait until she was five, and they would all participate.

Five! Two and a half years. By five, they wrote, the character was formed. Curie would be jelled and ready. She could be influenced but not transformed. Lily watched Curie play, aghast. Formed? At five? The little mite who chattered to herself, who walked on plump and sturdy legs with chance and change waiting around every corner – formed? At five? The information shocked her. She was the ignorant one, not them. No one had told her her darling would be formed by five, formed by her.

The importance of her own influence overwhelmed her. She joined the local library and read up on childcare. She was not frustrated, after all, in her desire for a sense of re-dedication and renewal at this juncture. She re-dedicated herself and renewed her sense of vocation. It became a sense of mission. Whatever happened in the future, she would always be the most important person in Curie's life. Her godmotherhood had begun.

Mike was left out for the present, but that brought relief as well as disappointment. He'd keep. She wasn't sure she wanted anyone – any relative – except herself allowed near Curie in these crucial years. She was also, suddenly, very busy. There was no laziness left in her. She zealously found playgroup and nursery in turn for Curie, she baked teacakes and entertained children to tea. She became known as a wonderful babysitter. Curie never lacked for company.

Curie flourished. She had constant devotion from Lily, and more erratic, haphazard attention from her Greenham aunts. She knew Bee was her mother, by a technicality she neither questioned nor fathomed. The knowledge was abstract. Lily was a daily reality and Bee a fortnightly or monthly one.

Her fifth birthday approached. The Greenham women arrived on the Day, bearing gifts, to take Lily and Curie to the seaside, where the ceremony was to take place. Curie wore a smart white smock. Lily's taste had changed during her years with Curie. She had educated herself in that way, too. She now dressed herself simply and well, though she indulged Curie's tacky alter ego, as well as her own, by sewing dolls' clothes as lacy and flouncy as she could make them.

Curie's birthday was in late August, but a cool wind blew as Lily led her by hand down the pebbly Brighton beach. They were taking her to the pier afterwards, for a treat.

The drama of total immersion was rendered more dramatic by the fact that Lily, dead white in a plain black swimsuit, immediately sank and failed to get up again. The blue felt beret she had insisted upon wearing right into the water (the dolls had had trailing mantillas) floated for a second and then, saturated, followed her. Curie, who could swim, thanks to Lily, shrieked and thrashed in her direction. Then one of the aunts jumped in, and Lily was rescued. They wanted her to rest and get her breath, but she insisted on carrying on, waterlogged as she was. After the baptism and kisses and hugs were over, she told them that she had once jumped into a swimming pool, as a child, which had just been emptied.

But her voice was vague, distracted, as she spun the yarn. She didn't really care whether they believed it, though she knew they would. Maybe it was true, maybe the world was the dry pool she was born into, that had put her off swimming forever.

She was watching Curie as she ran on the pebbles and laughed at the gulls. Something was coming to an end. Curie was starting school in a few days. Lily's central custodianship was over. She would begin the long, slow decline into shadow, as other influences stole Curie's attention. She wept over the glass of wine in her hand. The books said she ought not to view it that way. It was change, that was all. But she had been so happy that it was difficult to imagine any change being for the better.

Loneliness, she identified. That's it. Loneliness will come back. She meant 'the' loneliness, her specific loneliness, which had specifically gone for these three and a half years, on a sort of leave of absence. She had forgotten that the reprieve was temporary, that it must come back. Of course she would stay with Curie, there was no question of any change there. She and Bee had discussed it. They were a family now.

But the hours loomed ahead, disorganized, unstructured. She could babysit, but it was Curie who made it a social occasion and not a chore, as she did the launderette. She was not enamoured of children in general, not unless they were in tandem wih Curie. She could read, but books were stale and secondhand now. If they held no love like hers for Curie, they were irrelevant, and if they did they were inadequate. Nowhere did she find her own feelings described, now that she knew them, and she could no longer live vicariously, in the feelings of others.

She resolved, finally, to ring Mike. She had told herself

she would do so once the milestone of the baptism was over. Maybe he would help somehow, be company for her. At least he would be a distraction, and she needed distraction. She was determined to allow no grudging shadow to fall across Curie's first day at school.

Mike's voice on the phone brought tears to her eyes. It sounded exactly the same. That voice reminded her of the loneliness, all right, so sharply she almost panicked and threw down the receiver. But she didn't. Instead she told him, somewhat coyly, that she had a child now, a child whose name was Curie.

'What kind of a Christian name is that,' he demanded crossly. 'Is she christened at all?'

'Yes, she is.' She had known he would ask. Superstitiously, she would never lie about a thing like that, so she had had to delay their reunion until it was done, or face his disapproval. 'She's named for Marie Curie.'

'Why didn't they name her Marie then and she'd be named for the Mother of God as well,' he said, rather oddly.

She wondered who he thought the 'they' were, and decided to ignore it. Most likely his pronouns were going, as Bridget's had gone.

'Why don't you come and see her,' she pressed gently.

'Yes, I'll come,' he readily mumbled. 'I'll come this very day if you'll offer me lunch. I can get off at lunchtime.'

'Grandfather's coming,' she told Curie. It sounded like something from *Heidi*, but she didn't know what else to call him. They shopped for lunch, laid the table, dressed, giggling and primping.

She is my daughter, Lily said mutinously, silently, to their reflections in the mirror as they hugged each other. They were wearing their baptismal dresses.

He'd be prompt, Lily guessed, as she bustled and fussed. The reunion was a kind of first meeting, as if they were strangers. Which they were.

Truth, she muttered over the potatoes. What is it? That

160

was Pilate's line. But the devil always got the best lines, Bridget said. How did she know?

Curie was chattering happily next door, to her dolls. Help me, mother, she prayed formally to Bridget. With the old bastard, she added, as if to curry favour.

Was it selfish to ask Bridget for help, now, when she was finally at rest? But she had been unable to proffer any, before. Maybe Lily could draw on the wit she remembered, the laugh she remembered before it grew sly or faraway. Maybe she could draw on the energy Bridget had once had, before it funnelled inwards and tore her from her bearings like a cyclone. Maybe now Bridget watched over daughters with comprehending eyes. At least she could spare Lily her own blindness, her own deafness. Please.

She tested the potatoes and the roast chicken with an authoritative skewer. This would be a reconciliation with both Bridget and Mike. She had forgiven them both, and she could expect their forgiveness in return, voiced by Mike. Their forgiveness could not be insignificant, or meaningless, though she was not sure what she had done, except grow, and leave the caravan, and become someone who was not Bridget or Mike. Maybe that was enough.

Curie wandered into the kitchen and took in the preparations. She loved visits and parties. She was used to playing hostess, with Lily, to her aunts and her mother. Now, though, there was someone or something a bit different expected. A man. Lily deliberately dropped a knife as they laid the table and explained that that meant a man was visiting. A spoon meant a child, a fork meant a lady. Curie just as deliberately dropped a succession of forks and spoons and itemized the mothers and children she anticipated. Curie had to talk her out of setting places for them.

Mike would be a worthwhile presence in Curie's life, if only to introduce her to masculinity, Lily reflected. As she was reflecting, the doorbell rang.

Mike boomed his hellos, loud as ever. He was greyer and

heavier, otherwise unchanged. He grabbed Curie and twirled her around in the air. She screeched, recognizing something a little more aggressive in his energy as he played with her, Lily thought. She had learned the words. But were they the right ones? She was an airplane, Curie cried ecstatically. She was Concorde.

Lily opened the bottle of wine he had brought. She hoped he would relax, that he wouldn't be too raucous with Curie all through lunch and take away her appetite, or give her indigestion.

He didn't. He himself ate with great appetite as he told Lily all about his job, his bedsit above the pub, and her sisters.

'They always ask about you,' he said reproachfully, 'and –' He stopped abruptly, and took a gulp of wine.

Lily waited.

'Never you mind, Lill,' he said gently, and stooped to pat Curie on the head.

Lily was perturbed. What did he mean, what was in his mind? He straightened up and looked across the chicken at her.

'Now, Lily,' he said awkwardly. 'I'm happy you've found yourself a good place, my dear, and I want you to make the best of it.'

She nodded, not looking at him. His words hung in the air, at an odd angle to their little family party. He got up and went to his jacket, which was hung on the newel-post at the bottom of the stairs. It assumed a sinister importance, a four-dimensional significance, as she watched him approach it, the post with the jacket on it, as if her fate somehow hung there, too.

As it did. He took a rolled-up magazine, a Sunday colour supplement, from the inside pocket, and put it down gently on the table in front of her. Bee's face looked up from the cover, in a bevy of Greenham women and police.

'Mummy,' Curie hurried over. She had watched the little

162

scene, drawn by a sense of its drama. She knew the picture well, and the others inside the magazine. She and Lily had been over the article many times. She thumbed through impatiently till she found it, and took it over to Mike.

'Mummy,' she said again. 'Annie, Susie,' she began pointing out the women she knew in the pictures.

Lily looked at Mike over Curie's head. He was smiling a pained smile.

'Joan brought it over,' he said simply. 'She read it and thought it must be the same Lily.'

It must be the same Lily – his words echoed in her head. But I'm not the same Lily, she wanted to say. I'm another Lily now, oh, please, don't spoil it.

He went on talking to Curie, admiring everyone, everything, she pointed out, exclaiming over the brave, pretty ladies. Lily almost smiled at the way he added 'pretty'. It was of a piece with his particular politics.

'All right, Lily,' he asked, looking over shrewdly. ''Tis better this way, you know, no more need for that – blarney,' he sighed.

She nodded. She felt drained and exhausted. She needed to escape from his all-seeing eye, to escape into the anonymous streets for a breathing space, to be alone with herself while she adjusted to the turn things had taken.

'I think I'll step out, if you'll stay for a minute or five,' she said to him, in the old way; only then it was Bridget she wanted him to babysit, relieving her.

He smiled. 'Sure, go ahead,' he said, a mite too heartily. He pressed a fiver into her hand and told her to buy some more wine, and something for the child.

She went out, closing the door behind her. Curie was quite sanguine about staying behind with Grandad. Lily felt a stab of jealousy. It was the novelty, she consoled herself.

Out in the street, she began to tremble. It was the reaction. The world had turned over another page on her, this time a literal one. She wasn't sure what it meant. She didn't know whether she was relieved or distraught. She was both. She was too many things at once, as if everything had caught up with her, not just this. Everything, or everyone. Her sisters, Mike, Bridget, Curie, all in one day, and stretching beyond them, Bee and the women at Greenham, and even the police in the picture, staring out at her as if they knew, too. History had caught up with her. She breathed in short, quick gasps as she came out of the off-licence clutching her bottle. Her eyes blurred and she closed them just for a second's relief from confusion and guilt, as she reminded herself that these things were no longer the staples of her inner life, that they were washed away. As she opened her eyes she had a mental image of the washing machines all whirling away in a row, like dervishes. The image merged with the rubbery squelch of the tyres that came down over her, the splash of wine in her face as the bottle exploded, and a sound like the churning of wash, a sort of pulpiness, a squeezing. But it was herself that was pulped and squeezed, she understood. There were faces and noises and pain, far away. Was it the bomb, she wondered as a siren blared, but no, it was an ambulance, thank God for that, or Bridget. It was only the end of Lily's world, not everyone's, not Curie's, or Bee's, or all the 'brave, pretty ladies'. Women, she corrected herself. Curie was safe with Mike, she remembered. Her mind raced as hands moved around her. She felt like Gulliver being laced by the Lilliputians as she was placed on a stretcher, or even like Christ being hoisted on the cross. It hurt that much. But she shook that image away as blasphemous. The baptism, she remembered. God willing, it would wash away all of her sins and all of her temporal punishment. Bridget, she must concentrate all her hope on Bridget, Bridget would plead for her, as she floundered in the water, as she was twisted inside like a load of washing, by the pain. 'M-other,' she murmured. She heard an exclamation, a cry, in answer, and turned eagerly in its direction.

164

'So you did know someone who believed in life after life,' Sophia said gently.

'Life after death.'

'But you called it – after-life.'

'The afterlife, it was called, meaning life after death.'

'I do not understand,' Sophia shrugged. 'Not at all. But it does not matter.' She went on rhythmically stroking Curie's ankle. 'Not to me. Only to Lily Ghost, and to you.'

She leaned forward and took a tear from Curie's face as if it were an insect she was loathe to kill. No more insects, Curie thought, and her tears came for real.

'She believed in it, all right,' she sobbed in Sophia's arms. 'She believed in a life after death, and a life after life, and any other kind of life.'

'And she was right, for you have lived them all. And she has, too, in you. There is much of Lily Ghost in you, Curie.' Sophia laughed suddenly. 'You funny old – old –' she searched for a word.

'Bird,' Curie supplied. 'Like the thing of the Hands and Feet, but alive. A flying animal.'

'But you are not a flying animal, Curie. You are – you are–'

165

'A child,' Curie said simply. 'Oh, Sophia, I wish I could tell you about the doll clothes!'

'Tell me.'

Curie described them, the long dresses with flounces and bustles and trains, the parasols and mantillas. Sophia listened and smiled, but her forehead puckered.

'But Curie, who could wear such small clothes?'

So she had to explain dolls. The pucker ironed out. Sophia nodded.

'Like the figures in the graveyard.'

'Maybe they were,' Curie said slowly. 'They were waxy and made-up, rather like corpses, to imitate life. Maybe we weren't as ignorant of death as I thought. Maybe we knew it all the time. Maybe we played with it, too.'

'Curie, you are sounding morbid. Lily Ghost was never –'

'She was very morbid, Sophia. She told me the story about that poor man who was buried alive and couldn't be canonized because he –'

Sophia shrugged and asked the meaning of 'canonized'.

'She must've told me that a million times,' Curie said when she had explained. 'Each time she made it more gory, until she had exhausted all the possibilities. He had clawed out his eyes, he had bitten off his fingers, he had –'

'Enough stealing Lily's stories,' Sophia said cheerfully. 'Shall we go on?'

They scattered Lily's ashes in the sea, where Curie had been baptized. Mike frowned when he understood their intention, but said nothing. It was their funeral.

Afterwards they drove back to the old apartment. There was the cake Lily had made two days before, and another in the freezer. They defrosted the second and ate the first, and again Mike frowned, but kept silent.

Then Bee began to discuss the sale of the flat, and he could keep silent no longer. 'Can't you see what you're doing to the child,' he burst out. This is her home that you're talking of selling. She's lost Lily. She's even lost Lily's cake.'

They looked down at their empty plates. It was true. Curie had eaten nothing. She was curled up asleep on Lily's bed when they looked for her. The aunts, sensing a dispute of some sort, left Bee and Mike on their own.

'You're quite right,' Bee acknowledged. 'What you don't know, of course, is that Lily was a sort of mother figure to me, too, and I feel I've lost her twice over because of the – things she said.'

'The lies,' Mike said heavily. 'Why not use the word? She suffered enough because of it. Lies. It's only a word, and who knows, in the end, what the truth is? Why does it have to be the literal everyday stuff, what about what's in dreams and books, who says that isn't true? Who says?' he demanded aggressively. 'I said,' he answered himself rhetorically, a second later.

He's giving a funeral oration, Bee realized.

'I said Lily's dreams were not the truth, and that killed her,' he pronounced. 'I sentenced her to literalness, and that to her was death. I might as well have – what harm was she doing at all?' He interrupted himself. 'What harm? To whom? Me? Is the literal truth so important to me, to me whose life is a trail of white lies like the trail of a snail in the grass? Was it so important to her mother, poor woman, who was born without the power to tell the truth apart from lies, black or white? Maybe Lily inherited her unfortunate condition. In that case,' he finished, refilling his glass, 'it may be just as well. She'd have ended up mad as a snake.'

Bee blinked.

'But what will you do now?' He asked her directly. 'Take the little one with you to camp, is it?'

'I suppose,' Bee filled her own glass. 'Though if I could – I'd go away for a while. To think.'

'I don't know that going away helps you to think,' Mike said thoughtfully. 'I used to do that. Then again –' he looked at her speculatively. 'I'll stay here with Curie, if you like. While you're gone. Till you decide what to do.'

Bee looked at him, blue eyes considering. She was inclined to trust him as she could not have trusted a younger man, though many women of her age did. They said young men were without the long-conditioned prejudices that beset their fathers. Bee looked at Mike, and thought how much he had learned.

Curie's voice floated from the bedroom.

'She's waiting for Lily. Looking for her,' Bee said brokenly.

'She found her,' Mike replied. 'She's the only one who

ever did. Lily was herself with Curie – and with you, too, more than you think,' he added, gallantly but also honestly.

'She just didn't trust me enough.'

'She hadn't learned trust. It wasn't a lesson that me and her mother could teach.'

'I'm going to take you up on your offer, Mike,' Bee announced. 'I must have some time to myself right now. And it will be good for Curie, to be with you.'

In the event, she was right. It was, at the very least, not bad for Curie to land with Mike, in the confusion that followed. He led a piratical sort of life of bustle and bluster. There was a great deal to distract Curie. She needed a great deal of distraction. They moved to the rooms above the pub. The time had come when it was simply impossible to stay in the flat. Lily had not come back, and then Bee had not come back. Mike took Curie and fled to the pub, to safety and anonymity. He was afraid of publicity, afraid for her life, terrified for her sanity. He cared for her as best he could, and if he occasionally went on a bender, at least he came back. Most important of all, perhaps, he had the good grace not to die until she was over eighteen, and then undramatically.

'Curie, you cannot just rush past it all like this,' Sophia grabbed her as if to stop her. 'You must say what happened to Bee.'

Curie nodded, and cleared her throat. 'I know. But it's very difficult, you see, because I don't really know. I know she went away to the countryside and took all of Lily's letters and notebooks with her. After she died they were taken by the police,' she added resentfully. 'She was thinking, mostly about Lily, I suppose.'

'Instead of you.'

'She went directly back to Greenham Common instead of to the flat where I was waiting for her. She had discovered something about Lily, something she wanted to share with the other women who had known her. She was

169

possessed by Lily's truth. She hurried from the bus stop to the Camp. She put her hands in her pocket and found Curie's mitten, left there the day of the funeral. She fingered it and drew it out. Suddenly she looked at the barbed wire in front of her. It was terribly quiet, much too quiet. She heard a dog somewhere, a mournful howl. Poor thing, she thought, and walked resolutely towards the gate, the barbed wire. Blue was her last thought, if it was a thought. It was the name of the gate, and the colour of the mitten. She managed to pin the mitten on the barbed wire as a great wave of pain overtook her. She was strangely calm as she felt herself fall. It had happened before, though she hadn't fallen, but then, she hadn't been climbing gates, either. She smiled at the thought, but the smile went wrong. That time she had heard a retort, a shot, and then her waters were broken and she was in labour, riding wave after wave of pain. They said she couldn't have heard it, but she had. This time, though, she was sinking beneath the waves, not riding them. The sound was the same. The mitten swam in front of her eyes and then it, too, sank.'

'Is that all, Curie?' Sophia asked.

'It's all I have to say.'

Sophia was silent.

'What do you think she found out about Lily?'

'How the hell do I know? She didn't live to say, to pass it on. *She* never had to tell her tale.'

'But she was going to.'

'To them. Not to me.'

'How do you know, Curie?' Sophia demanded. 'How do you know it wasn't all for you?' When Curie remained silent, Sophia went on, more and more certainly as she found her voice.

'I think she discovered that Lily Ghost was both a nun and a nurse, as much as there is such a thing as a nun and a nurse. And also that she was something else, Curie, as you are, as Bee herself was. A storyteller. I think she recovered her own truth, the truth she told when she claimed the Fairchilds had abandoned her in her pregnancy. It may not have been literally true, any more than Lily had literally entered a convent or nursed in a hospital, but perhaps they rejected her, just the same, just as Lily took her vows of poverty, chastity and obedience, and nursed so many things in her heart, so that her nursing of you was only the last –'

'The last and the least, I suppose?' Curie's eyes glittered dangerously. 'Sophia, I don't think I asked you for an ending to this chapter, or an interpretation.'

'Any more than Bee asked you,' Sophia flashed back. 'But she had given you life and couldn't stop you using it, any more than you can stop me. I think Mike was right, too, that Bee discovered for herself that you had found Lily, really found her. But he only saw half of it, because Lily had found you, too, you were her foundling, and Bee realized that too, when she thought about Lily and re-read her letters, and then she wanted to be with you, to discover you for herself. I think she hurried to Greenham Common to say goodbye, to leave your mitten waving goodbye, because she would have to leave Greenham for a time, to be with you. But she was prevented.'

'Oh, Sophia, you child. You've reinvented the Hollywood ending, and I am not going to explain. You want me to feel good –'

'Curie,' Sophia interrupted sternly, 'Why do you not consider this idea?'

'Because,' Curie began, but it was too late to stop the idea that was so much more than an idea from taking shape in her mind. Bee had rushed to the base to make her farewells because she had resolved to be with her daughter, away from Greenham; or she stuck the mitten there as a pledge to return, bringing Curie with her. Was that not exactly what she, Curie, had suspected, was that not the suspicion she had had to suppress, in her biography and in herself? Because otherwise Bee would have to be thawed

171

out and loved. The glass would shatter and the terrible alarm bells sound, of love and longing and grief. As they sounded now, as Curie wept in Sophia's arms.

'But how did you know all that,' she demanded tremulously, as her sobs subsided. 'Sophia, how could you know it?'

Sophia shrugged her characteristic shrug. 'It came from what you did not say,' she said shrewdly.

'But where did you learn about silence? From the Potters?'

'Curie,' Sophia said crossly, tossing her head, 'the Potters did not teach us everything. There are things we taught them.'

'Just like you and me.'

Sophia nodded. 'Now there is something I wish you to explain, Curie. It is this "cry wolf" thing.'

Curie nodded in turn, relieved to resume her role of teacher. 'Once upon a time,' she began, 'there was a little girl who was left all day, every day, in charge of some sheep.' Curie explained sheep as best she could, and was forced to laugh as Sophia became a sheep in ingenious pantomime.

'It is the only way to understand,' Sophia puffed, getting up off the floor.

'Sophia, you child,' Curie said again. 'Never mind, it's a child's story. You'll have to get down on the floor again, and do the wolf,' she sighed, and explained the wolf. 'Greedy, hungry, devouring,' she itemized.

Sophia blinked. 'Just like the sheep, with their endless nibble, nibble on the grass.'

'Yes, but the wolf devours flesh, and has great big teeth,' Curie explained, 'and is wild and strong and fierce, not silly and meek.'

Sophia, eyes crackling with wolf energy, got down again on the floor and snapped and snarled around Curie's hastily withdrawn ankles.

'The little girl was told to call for help if ever the wolf

172

appeared by crying "wolf, wolf". So she called, just to see what would happen.'

'Very wise of her,' Sophia nodded.

'What on earth do you mean, Sophia? You don't understand. There was no wolf.'

'No,' Sophia said equably. 'She was testing the alarm system.'

'Sophia, where did you get such language?'

'Why, from you, Curie, where else?'

'The little girl cried wolf again and again when there was no wolf nearby,' Curie continued, 'until one day a wolf did appear, snarling and salivating, and she cried in vain. "Wolf, wolf," the little girl cried, but no one came, because they knew she was a liar.'

'But she was not,' Sophia cried, 'she was not! Oh, Curie, what happened to her?'

'She was eaten by the wolf, as she deserved to be.'

'As she *what*?' Sophia demanded.

'Sophia, the moral of the story is not to tell lies, not to cry wolf, that is, set off false alarms.'

'Now I understand.' Sophia stood abruptly. 'Now I see. This is what they accused the women of, at Greenham Common? I do not think you understand this story either, Curie. I do not think you have listened, or maybe you have listened too many times. Who are you to say the little girl was lying, or that her alarms were false? The little girl is real and the wolf is real. In the end it eats her. Maybe it came every time and ran away when it heard the people approaching. Did you not say it was a crafty animal?'

Curie nodded mutely.

'Well, then. Or maybe the little girl had visions of the wolf that would come some day, visions so real that she had to cry out. Maybe she was a prophet. Or maybe,' Sophia said enthusiastically, 'maybe she didn't cry wolf, maybe she called the wolf.'

'What?'

173

'"Wolf, wolf," could be a call. Maybe the wolf was her friend. They were both lonely and they played together. But one day maybe the wolf came in a pack, and then was not her friend, but friend of the other wolves, who made it choose. It was afraid, and it chose the wolves, but I do not think the little girl cried out, that day. I think they made that up later, to excuse themselves for leaving her alone, poor little girl on the hillside with the boring, silly sheep.' Sophia baa-ed fatuously.

'Did I say hillside?' Curie looked at her curiously. 'Where did you get the hillside?'

Sophia shrugged. 'It was there, in my mind, like your window,' she said. 'I made it up, like you did. Did you think you were the only one who could do such things? And isn't that what the little girl did when she cried wolf, isn't that what everyone does when they make something in their minds, with their minds?'

Curie stared at her. 'Imagination is a child crying wolf,' she said softly. 'Yes, why not? As you say, Sophia, the child is real and the wolf is real and the child is ultimately devoured, by the wolf or by the fear of those who do not listen, either to the cry or to the silence. The cause of death is lack of imagination. And, yes, I too suspect that the wolf is harmless, alone. I suspect that the wolf comes to play with the child. I, too, suspect a conspiracy between them, the lonely child and the lone wolf.

'But sometimes the wolf is not a wolf, but a pack. I suspect that then the child does not cry "wolf", but the pack cries "child", and the grownups' blood runs cold. They stay at home and hide, and the alibi is made up later.'

The men were not men, but a pack. The women only realized it after they had begun their stories for the second time, when the signals had gone.

First they each took a long, deep breath, held it and exhaled it. They had prepared for this moment as women prepare for labour. They had practised the same deep and shallow breathing, the same panting, the same repetition during what is called the transition stage of labour, between the onset of contractions and hard labour. They knew from their reading that this stage is irritating and exhausting. They knew from their reading that the irritation and exhaustion come not from pain but from confusion. It is a chaotic stage, lengthy and muddled, between a dramatic beginning and a climactic end. It is the stage that most resembles a lifetime. There is a technique for dealing with the transition stage. It is repetition, or ritual. Monks and drunks engage in it too. Drunks favour the repetition of *Danny Boy* or *Auld Lang Syne* or a ballad to which they give their own words, a song of destiny with or without a tune. Monks tend towards Gregorian chant, while others, temporary conscripts, veer more towards *Amazing Grace*, or *Onward, Christian Soldiers*.

The women released their breaths and plunged into their stories with all the despairing determination of women in labour, chanting *Ten Green Bottles*. They would go on telling their tales until the transition stage was over, and hard labour began.

They delivered their tales to the accompaniment of footsteps down the metal corridors. The men listened not to them but to the footsteps. They listened for a signal from the pack, as they had listened all along.

The stories went on for a third and fourth and fifth time as the women were taken from the bunkers, bundled into vehicles, and driven away. They went on for a sixth and a seventh time, each in her separate, anonymous car, until they stood together in an airplane hangar and saw that hard labour was about to begin.

'You thought we were really stupid,' the general sneered. 'Really stupid,' considering, his very pink face reddening as he considered. 'And you were right.'

The women looked at him. They listened intently. He was a powerful speaker. The airplane hangar had excellent acoustics. It was a setting that commanded attention, a theatre of sorts. As the general spoke, the one plane in the huge, draughty hangar was packed with eskimo suits like rustling shadows, food and drink like the offerings once buried with the dead.

'We were stupid.' The general's face was mottled. 'You almost had us. You had us, except for one little slip-up.' He grinned. His face was pink and white once more. 'Guess God was on our side,' he said modestly. 'It seems one of you ladies just can't keep a secret.'

They stared at him, deliberately blank.

'What are you going to do with us?' Davy asked tersely.

'I'm glad you asked me that,' he was genial now. He had found his rationale: God. Heads would roll, of course, but that, too, would be God's doing. 'I was wondering how to bring up that very topic. It's delicate, very delicate. But you're not, luckily,' he glanced at them, only once and very fleetingly. 'Luckily, because where you're going is no place for the delicate.'

'I'm pregnant,' India said coldly.

'Congratulations.' The general answered her in the same tone, without a look. 'You can figure out who the traitor is while you're on your way,' he suggested, almost conversationally. 'It's a long way, and there ain't no movie.'

'If you think we believe your filthy lies,' Davy began.

He waved her aside, and shrugged. 'Doesn't matter to me what you believe,' he said cheerfully. 'If anything. I know the truth.'

Afterwards they could not agree as to whether he had said 'I know the truth' or 'I own the truth'. They decided that the two statements had the same meaning for him.

They were bundled aboard the plane, not brutally, just indifferently, as if they were dead or worse, had never been alive. They shouted protests and curses at first and then, when they were buckled securely into their seats and there was no possibility of reprieve or escape, they fell silent.

176

It was only when they had been airborne for an hour or more that they spoke. They re-entered their voices cautiously. It had been necessary to send those voices out to storm and swarm the general, the men on the tarmac, to sting and leave whatever inflammation of conscience they could. Before then, in the bunkers, in the metal corridors, in the military vehicles, it had been necessary to send their voices out to hold the silence like an icy road. Now they expected those voices to be changed, like boys' grown into men's, or castrati, but they were only voices, and they alternately stormed and held the silence, still.

They talked about the world they were leaving behind. They acknowledged as they had not done before, that that world was in tatters. Never before in recent history could they have been so unceremoniously flung away. Disappearances of the sort common in other places had begun to occur in England. They had realized it before, without allowing themselves to react, except in accordance with the common reaction, a phenomenon as disturbing in itself as were the disappearances. Those who vanished were unstable. They had a morbid streak, a romantic tendency. This was usually true, according to the definitions of conventional wisdom, each of which was a comfortable cul-de-sac.

They were given bread and water. They drank and chewed greedily, giggling over the cartoon character of their prison fare. Altitude and exhaustion had done their work. They were lightheaded, giddy.

'Let me tell you about my affair,' India said, when they had wolfed down everything put before them. 'That'll make you laugh.'

'Oh, yes,' Ruth said enthusiastically. 'And then I'll tell you about mine. I'm pregnant too.'

'Maybe it's the same one,' Davy growled. 'The same man, I mean.'

'They'd be sisters,' India said softly.

'They'd better be sisters,' Ruth said shortly.

'I met him at the Star and Garter,' India began. 'I was sitting there having a drink, establishing my village presence, and he came up and started chatting me up. Good, I thought, more credibility. I wonder what I do next? I just kept smiling and nodding and trying to agree with everything he said, except when it seemed safe not to, in keeping with my character, that is. He talked mostly about his car and football and things like that, and as I didn't know anything about them anyway, it was easy to agree. Then we went home to bed.'

'Just like that?' Clare demanded.

India nodded.

'You always were a fast worker,' Ruth said affectionately. 'I remember back in the old days when we still brought people home. If you brought the same woman back two nights running, it was probably a mistake. Alcoholic amnesia.'

'I wasn't that bad,' India said modestly. 'It was just a phase, anyway. But this –' she paused, then went on gloomily. 'Well, it was all right for a week or two, and then he told me he was sorry but he couldn't respect me, because I had slept with him so quickly. And he didn't like sleeping with someone he didn't respect, though he liked sleeping with me, of course.'

'Of course,' Davy muttered.

'What did he look like, Ind,' Clare asked.

'He was very pretty,' India said, more gloomily. 'I think what I liked best was his green hair, which stood up in fantastic spikes which he made with soap –'

'With soap,' Davy spluttered. 'D'you mean he was a punk?'

'Oh, yes,' India nodded.

'A puritanical punk,' Ruth sighed. 'Well, they weren't so different after all. Mine was a puritanical married man. You know what they get off on, puritans? Guilt,' she concluded. 'Mine loved his guilt, much more than me.'

178

Curie broke the silence. 'I think I –' she faltered.

Davy cut in quickly. 'We're going to play Twenty Questions,' she said brusquely. 'And after that we're going to have a sexual fantasies competition. And after that –' she shrugged, 'we'll think of something.' She flashed Curie a hard look that said: shut up.

They arrived, or at least landed. There was nothing to see but snow. By unanimous unspoken consent, they refused to leave the plane. They were lifted by the pilot, still goggled and mute, and the surly co-pilot, and jettisoned.

'Maybe we're being taken to another planet,' Clare had conjectured, in mid-flight.

'In a plane?' Davy had sneered.

But then they considered the feeling behind the statement and decided it was backwards. The world behind them became another planet as they looked over their shoulders to remember it. They had not known it.

Now, though, they were in another dimension of the unknown, and Clare's projection seemed to face forwards again. They could be on another planet, and perhaps they were. As they rolled upright, with difficulty, they too were strange in their dark, warm suits. They had been hoisted into them, one by one, before landing. The operation had been oddly upsetting, as four of them sat, buckled in, helpless to assist the fifth who was being outfitted in the thick new clothes. It was as if she were being raped, the observers and the observed both felt. The element of coercion was the same, if not that of invasion. Afterwards, as they sat uncomfortably in their suits, they were embarrassed with each other, until they discussed what had happened.

Now they stretched and stumbled in their moon-suits. There was a soft thud and they turned to see the pilot coming towards them.

'It's Goggles,' Davy said hoarsely. 'Wonder what she wants?'

The goggles came off. A hand reached up and ruffled her own hair, like a transvestite ending a performance with the dexterous admission: I'm a man. Except that in this case, it was the opposite admission.

She bowed and laughed into their faces. Then she searched through the snow that fell so fast and thickly it seemed to hang in the air like lace curtains, until she found Curie among their padded figures.

Curie cringed away as the pilot stopped in front of her. She pressed in close, a daunting figure in her Air Force uniform. Then she leaned forward and kissed Curie hard, on the mouth. She backed away, and kept backing, and as she backed she took a hand and wiped it across her mouth. Then she flung the invisible patina of Curie's lips away into the snow, turned on her heel and ran back towards the plane, now revved and waiting.

'Come on,' Davy shouted, the first to recover.

They raced after her, but it was too late. She waved from her window as the plane buzzed away.

Only one of them had spent the entirety of the flight preoccupied with the information the general had imparted. The others assumed it was a tactic meant to destroy their bonding, to fracture their loyalty and fraction their chances of survival.

Davy bent down and picked up a back pack from the snow. 'We walk,' she shouted. 'We don't stand still, and we don't think. Curie, you lead.'

Curie tried to speak.

181

'You lead,' Davy said savagely.

Curie nodded dumbly. She understood. She had singled herself out and so she would remain singled out, and alone. They needed someone to do it, though ordinarily they would not have, could not have, burdened anyone with the isolation of leadership, with the punishment of it. In her case, the punishment fit the crime.

They walked. They wandered, but they didn't call it that and so it was not that. They walked, with purpose, nowhere, until they found a cave, and that became their destination. It was overnight shelter. They slept there, all except Curie, who alternated between insomnia and nightmare.

In the morning, they had to decide whether to leave the cave or continue on through it. Curie wanted to leave. Davy disagreed.

'Think the way they think,' Davy insisted. 'They think we'd leave. They think we'd be afraid of it. That's why they left us here. If the way to survive is through the cave, the odds are we won't find it.'

'What if the way to die is through the cave,' Clare asked. 'It may collapse on us, or –'

'Or anything,' Ruth threw in. 'But I still feel we should go through it, and I think we proceed on what we feel because there isn't anything else. India?'

India nodded. 'Through the cave. Curie leads.'

Curie's insomnia continued. Getting out of the cave was her obsession as sleep is an insomniac's obsession. Sometimes she tried to forget about getting out as the insomniac tries to forget sleep, in order to ambush it. Sometimes she tried to feel herself on the brink of getting out, as the dreamer pinches herself to bring about wakefulness.

The cave darkened and deepened. There was a hissing sound, at first far off, then closer. Curie felt the cave to be a living thing, like a dragon. It was somehow segmented. She was not Jonah and it was not a whale. It was reptilian, not mammalian.

182

Its sides shrunk so that she must touch them. They were greasy and sticky at once, as if coated with mucus. The cave might sneeze or puke them into space, might shit them into the earth or simply absorb them into itself.

The ceiling came down and down. Curie crept, then slithered on her belly. It was like a downwards spiral through evolution, until, pulling herself forwards with pelvic thrusts, braced on claw-like hands, she was less than human.

It was not *like* anything. She did not think, I am not Jonah, I am experiencing the seven ages backwards. I am in the throes of birth, death, initiation. She thought nothing. Whatever she went through was gone through as a body. She had lost her mind. Her body was her mind. It grunted and creaked. There were no words. The word was made flesh.

It seemed that they were moving, evolving, together, the cave and the women, the stone dragon and the women who were themselves a little, segmented dragon, clawing and scraping at the larger one. It allowed its caverns to be clawed and scraped because it had no choice. It was immensely powerful, but helpless. It had been in existence for centuries, changed and moulded by infinitesimal shiftings of light, water and dirt. The light wormed here and the dirt followed, the water stilled here and made a pool which the light found and the dirt did or did not enter. Patterns and fungis appeared on rock faces. Water reacted to light, and to soil, with sound that would be called music, if there were words.

Curie had been a part of the light, going into an alien darkness. Now she was part of the darkness, a piece of the pattern, or orchestration. She forgot getting out. She was folded in. The darkness was like blood, a flowing redness, velvety and unperfumed except for a vague fungal smell, like orchids or mushrooms.

183

Then it was cold. They were dashed underwater and they struggled upwards and joined together to right India, who was swept down longer. They formed a chain to resist the swashbuckling current that dragged at their thighs. They waded upstream through the underground river, breathless, intoxicated with cold. The water tore at them to go back, the current demanded they go back, into the dark. They refused, and when there was light at last they grasped it like a rope.

They poured out of the cave like a waterfall, laughing as they rolled down the hill. They were light-hearted, punch-drunk with relief and gratitude. When they reached level ground they sat up slowly, stretching like dreamers. Then the laughter died on their lips.

It was silent. Utterly, icily silent. There were shadows, and as they leaned closer, as they stood up and approached, the shadows loomed and took on density without life, like statues. They were white of skin, these people, white as marble, and still. Around their feet milled other creatures, neither shadows nor statues but strange, small creatures, furred and whiskered. Each one, it seemed, was different from the rest.

'The Potters,' breathed Sophia.

These small children, for that is what they were, broke the silence to explain to the women what had happened. While they were fighting their way through the cave, within forty-eight hours of the sham enacted for their benefit, the reality had come.

Their first reaction was to rub their eyes and giggle. From nightmare to waking and back again was a journey so frequent they were beginning to feel like commuters. But

185

this they could not incorporate, could not absorb, and they began to question the children instead of trying.

But their parents, for that, they understood, was who the strange white-faced ones were, what had happened to them?

The women were led to yet another cave, this one clean and almost comfortable, except for a strange atmosphere of mingled anarchy and constraint they did not understand. The little ones scurried to feed them as they spoke. They knew well how to serve. They had always cared for their parents, had never, in fact, been children at all, despite their small stature and short years.

The children were the results of experiments. Their parents were political prisoners, of various persuasions, selected for their intelligence and fitness as well as for their crimes, to participate in what had become a secret cold war more terrible in its way than the arms race itself. It was a race to develop a master race that would survive the holocaust the superpowers knew was coming. Genders were mixed and blended, reserving the power of procreation, and the work was now complete; the Potters would survive. What the leaders did not foresee was that their own arrangements would prove insufficient, that they themselves would perish. The surviving race would not reveal, ever, to which side they had supposedly belonged. They knew both languages, because their parents did.

Their parents had had to watch as the experimenters toyed with their flesh. They had had to submit to terrible inseminations and matings from which they turned with horror. They had not ceased to turn back, to look towards the world they loved, the world they had sought in their different ways to protect, which they knew would be destroyed. They had turned to salt. Hence their whiteness, their silence.

The children described what they had heard before the radios went dead. It was, they said in their precocious vocabulary, an orgy of destruction. Missiles mounted the air from every nation known to possess them, and others besides. It was the last chance to prove you did not have to lie down and take it, though you did, as you always had. It was the last denial.

And now, the children said, they would retire in favour of the women, they would become children. The women were a godsend. They might even be gods. The little ones helped with the burial of their parents' stiff forms, for they stood as they were till they died, almost all, not quite. A remnant remained. The children evolved their own strange version of childhood, which involved playing in the grave-yard and tending the graves, while the women began to evolve their own motherhood, of these children, their own children, and GOB.

But first there were confessions. Clare's was a surprise to everyone, told on a dull grey evening when they were sick with exhaustion and grief from the day's burying and trying to talk to the motionless salt figures that remained upright. The children told them the effort was useless, but they could not desist.

'I think I should confess,' Clare said looking around at them, slumped in their makeshift seats. The winter had not yet come though the children predicted it. It was the reason for their fur.

Curie looked at her. 'Surely that's my line,' she said indignantly.

'Everyone knows what you've got to confess,' Davy told her with affectionate scorn.

She turned hungrily towards the voice, but Davy had turned away. They kept Curie at bed's length. She had no shortage of affection, but was unable to persuade herself into a passionate embrace with any of them, and that not from any hostility on their part. Quite the contrary. They wanted Curie to survive. The Potters, children that they were, had told them that part of the secret of survival was to refrain from passing any contaminated fluids during the danger period. Body fluids, that is. That was the constraint, perhaps, that the heads of government had found themselves unaccountably unable to bear. Perhaps they had found themselves in a frenzy of need, unprepared for the exigency precisely because they had been out of touch with their needs for so long.

The others had all been contaminated and inter-contaminated before the children remembered to mention that sex was to be strictly avoided. But Curie had been left out, first as punishment, and then as something else; punishment in another form, perhaps. She could threaten, blackmail or cajole no one, Founding Mother or Potter, to break the sanction.

So she subsided in the face of Davy's continued coldness which was not coldness, and let Clare speak first. When they heard her confession, she refected dolefully, they would know how perfectly their punishment fitted her crime.

'Remember that Sunday I came in from a political meeting and proposed Scheherazade,' Clare began.

'How could we forget it,' Davy said caustically. 'Do tell.'

'Well,' Clare went on, 'you,' she turned to Davy, 'gave me the idea of politics, you see, I mean the idea of pretending that it was a political group I'd joined.'

'You mean it wasn't?' Davy asked, intrigued. 'What the hell was it?'

Clare snickered, then laughed outright. 'It was the biggest bunch of lunatics you'd ever want to see,' she roared. 'End-of-the-worlders all, doomsday merchants.'

'But the date,' Ruth pressed unbelievingly. 'The date you said your intelligence had sussed –'

'It wasn't intelligence, darling,' Clare threw back. 'It was numerology, scientology, astral travelling, the tarot, palmistry, prophecy, pendulums, every sort of weird and wonderful thing you could think of except intelligence.'

'And it was almost right,' India said softly.

They sat awed by the accident, or coincidence, until Curie cleared her throat and spoke.

'It seems we're saved by our sins, not by our acts of virtue,' she said smoothly.

They looked at each other and grinned.

'All right,' Curie snapped. 'I'll just tell you right out. I had an affair with the pilot. Well, I was angry,' she wailed, 'at all of you, because you wouldn't sleep with me, back at the church.'

The triangle had dissolved upon the founding of Scheherazade by Clare, upon the founding of Clare by Clare. Clare had drifted into India's arms, Davy into Ruth's, and Curie was left out.

'Oh come on, Curie,' Davy said, 'if you're going to confess, confess. You had an affair with the pilot and you told her about Scheherazade, right?'

Curie nodded.

'She was a pilot. In the American Air Force.'

Curie nodded.

'You weren't betraying *us* with your handsome young captain in her shiny uniform, Curie. Think. You were betraying Bee Fairchild and everything she stood for. You were taking the first chance you had to disown her as you felt she'd disowned you. Remember that day we met?' She went on, passionate to prove her point as Curie continued to look blank, 'Remember how angry you were? And then it just went away, and there was no sign of it in your book, though a little of it crept into the window, in a fungal sort of way.'

'I don't remember,' Curie said wearily. 'I don't know what we're talking about and I don't know why, after everything that's happened. This is all irrelevant.'

'Curie,' Clare said in a low, intense voice, 'this is why things happen. This is why we're here. Because of your affair with the pilot.'

'Which saved us,' India remarked. 'Like Clare's lunatics saved us.'

'Yes, but why save me?' Curie demanded. 'Why can't I be with you, and go with you? And why did you leave me alone then, in the church?'

'We thought you needed to be alone,' Davy said flatly. 'To see it at last. I guess we only made you angrier.'

'But it worked out,' India said. 'It worked out.'

'Not for me,' Curie said wanly. 'I'm left behind again.'

'That's enough self-pity,' Davy said briskly. 'We have too much to do before we die. We can't leave you to map out the whole of the new world.'

'But Curie, the babies of Ruth and India,' Sophia begged, 'What of them?'

'They were born healthy,' Curie replied, 'except for a certain slowness, a fortuitous slowness in a way, for it helped them to get on with the small group of old ones who had somehow survived, eventually to breed with them and be –'

'Us, the M-others,' Sophia finished with a pleased wriggle. 'And the mothers, the four mothers, died?'

'Very peacefully,' Curie replied, almost bitterly. 'Very quietly. I nursed them all.'

'And so you were the nurse and the nun in the end, Curie,' Sophia said playfully, gathering Curie close. 'And what, may I ask, was her name?'

'Whose name? Oh, Sophia, why should it be like this? Why should they lie in Potter's Field and not I, not the Judas, why?'

'Because there was something you had to do, and you could not die until you had done it,' Sophia replied. 'And you cannot die now either, she added hastily, 'because there is still something else you must do. What was her name?' She repeated insistently.

'Whose name?'

'The pilot's.'

'Judy,' Curie said absently. 'What can there possibly be left for me to do now?'

'Curie, you are so stupid it is wonderful that you survived. I shall forgive you,' Sophia said judiciously. 'I shall forgive you this affair because otherwise you would not have survived, any one of you, and maybe she knew that.'

'Who?'

'Judy. Now, Curie –' Sophia sniffed the air suspiciously. 'Curie, what is that strange smell?'

Curie was jolted out of her daze by the question. She raised her head and sniffed, too, then ran to the opening and out into the wasteland. 'It isn't a smell, Sophia, it's cold, it's –' She lifted her hand and looked at it. 'It's snow, it's winter. It's come back, like a sign from them, from the four of them,' she said in her excitement, 'a signal that they've forgiven me, that time can be complete again now. Oh, Sophia,' she breathed as Sophia came to stand next to her and stare at the white-on-white blur in the air, 'there's so much to do. A whole new vocabulary to learn, a vocabulary of keeping warm, and oh,' she laughed wildly, 'so many things to do. Build snow – snow-M-others! and throw snowballs. But most important of all,' she went on, rubbing her hands together with anticipation, 'most of all there is the study of this, to find out why it has come about. The theology of it. Is it the gods?' she demanded. 'Restoring the lost season because what was lost has been restored here in the Gods of the Body? Memory,' she rushed on. 'Memory has been restored, and with it clarity and futurity of another order altogether. Is it the gods sending this snowfall like manna? Or does it come about automatically, is there no connection between what happens and what we do? No,' she shoved her own speculation aside, 'No, it cannot be coincidence, not unless we have misunderstood the nature of coincidence. We must meditate, we must discover, the relationship between mind and world.'

191

'Curie.' Sophia faced her. 'Shut up.' She began to move towards her, threateningly.

Curie backed up, into the little hut, till her thighs touched the bed and she toppled over onto it.

'We are both going to play in the snow, now,' Sophia said firmly. 'Do you understand? Because now you must make up for lost time, Curie, and you must meditate above all on the nature of love. Do you understand?'

'Love?' Curie asked in a thin small voice. 'Are you sure you are not crying wolf, Sophia?'

'Oh, but I am Curie, I am,' Sophia said joyfully. 'Maybe at last you understand your own story?'